Crazy Deja Vu

By

Lauresa Tomlinson

Young of Heart Publishing
P.O. Box 2274
Mckinleyville, CA 95519

2019

Introduction

Have you ever wanted to be a mind reading fly on the wall and watch someone's life fly by as it were? This is your chance. Rita is a young female living in Queens, New York. Her greatest adventure started mid-March 1997.

There are so many questions and such crazy answers. Has anything like this ever happened to you?

Come along while we play the part of a hidden reporter in her adventure.

Crazy Deja Vu

Chapter One

I awoke with my mind racing through all that had happened yesterday. I have so many questions, and really have no idea where to start looking for the answers.

I had thought about trying to dismiss the whole day. But it hadn't worked in the past.

The alarm just went off and I have to get up and get ready to go to work. While dressing, I caught myself wishing I could go to work and find out that this whole thing was just a crazy dream.

Let me start over so you will know what happened... I think...

It all started yesterday. I was at work

and everything was going great. I work in a small cafe on the main street of our community called "The Rooster Cafe". We serve all the locals and the same groups that come in each day for almost the same thing each time. There have been a lot of times I wished something would happen to make my life exciting.

Well, okay, a few days ago, Charlie, (my boss), decided to go shopping for something different or strange. He said we needed to have something to hang on the wall to make The Rooster Café stand out.

"If we are different then maybe we could get more business." He said.

'Okay, well maybe that will work, I don't know, I hope so.' I thought.

Next morning, Charlie came in toting what looked to be a really large painting. It was all covered up so no one could see it, until he decided to show us.

We were all standing around the painting in a half circle after work when he

took off the covering. Everyone else agreed
that if this painting didn't at least get
comments from the customers then they
didn't know what it would take.

As for myself, I was speechless, I
couldn't move for a few moments. I could
swear I had seen this painting somewhere
before. It felt as if I was the one who painted
it. It's almost like an itch in the back of your
mind that you can't reach. I'd lived in this
area for the last twenty years (most of my
life) and I'd never drawn anything much
less painted. I didn't even know if I could. I
have a good imagination and can picture
things in my mind, but as far as putting
them on paper, I had never really tried.

Well, at any rate, it's another morning
and my coffee is ready and the clock says I
only have time to catch the bus and get to
work.

*"OH NO!" 'Where are my keys? I can't
miss the 8:00 bus or I will be late'* "Ahh good!
There they are."

"Come on Anna, time to go play with your friends. Be a good girl today, stay out of trouble. OK?" I said as I placed her on the front steps. *'She is my good friend and tomorrow is her birthday.'* She is a beautiful calico cat with bright burnt orange and black strangely shaped markings.

It takes me about thirty minute to get to work. This was the closest apartment I could find for the money I have, and it's not all that bad. I know most of the people in the area and it's a pretty good neighborhood.

"Hi George, how are you today?" I asked while putting my token in the coin box. He's the bus driver on this route.

"Great Rita, How are you doing today? You looked like you were pretty shaken up yesterday evening." He said with a smile.

"I feel better this morning. Yesterday was crazy." I said, turning to find my best friend and the seat she always saved for me.

"Hey Rita, I heard you guys have a new look added to the café yesterday. What do you think?" Nell yelled from the back of the bus.

"Well it's different, that's all I'm going to say. You'll have to come by and see for yourself." I said on my way back to her.

"So you're not going to tell me what it's a picture of?" she coaxed.

"No, cause it is really hard for me to put into words." I said sitting down next to her. "It feels really funny to me, the painting I mean."

"What do you mean?" she asked.

We were the only ones sitting in the back half of the bus right now. We live close to the beginning of the bus route. Nell's a good friend and knows all kinds of weird things that most other people wouldn't even dare think of.

Sometimes when we talk on the bus we talk in code, you know, like as if we are talking about a movie we'd seen or a book we'd read. That way no one else thinks we're crazy.

"Well, yesterday when Charlie took the cover off the painting and showed it to everyone. I had this real funny feeling in the pit of my stomach. And when the others said they liked the painting and thought it was a great choice, it made me feel real good, like as if I was the one who painted it. I even had the feeling I had seen it before. Does that sound crazy or what?" I questioned.

"No, not really" she said as she laughed.

"What's so funny?" I asked.

"Well things are happening in this world and all around us, that only a few know about and they are really hard to explain." she said looking straight at me. "You will understand more as time goes on. And I can help you here and there. But for now don't worry about it, just explore the feelings." she instructed.

"Okay, if you say so. This is my stop. I'll see you this evening on the way home." I said.

"See you later George." I yelled while waving at him as I pushed opened the back door on the bus.

I am looking forward to it." Nell said as we waved at each other and I got off the bus.

Nell works downtown near the courthouse. So she had to ride the bus about another four miles.

The bus lets me off about half a block from the cafe. Most days I enjoyed the short walk, but this morning I felt a little confused.

'Nell said to explore my feelings, so I need to keep that in mind and not let my feelings take over my thoughts.'

There's the cafe, I really like that sign.

Charlie wanted to change it a while back and we all talked him out of it.

"Hi Joy!" I called out as I walked into the café.

Joy works with me on Tuesdays and Thursdays.

"Oh hi Rita, Did you see the painting we have on the wall now?" she asked.

'Yes, Charlie brought it in yesterday." I informed her.

"It's really strange. I was told its two painting in one. I like the idea of seeing

things that change when up close. Don't
you?" She said looking at the painting,
while tilting her head to one way and then
another.

"Yeah, I like it a lot." I said while
pulling my hair up and securing it in place, I
put on my apron as I walked out close to
where she was standing.

We both stood there looking at the
painting for a few minutes. "Have you

gotten a chance to see it from across the room?" I said.

"Not yet, we have stayed pretty busy all day so far." She answered as she finished clearing the table and walking back toward the kitchen.

Joy fit her name most of the time. She enjoyed laughing and sometimes in the afternoon we would get a laughing streak going and it would last all the way through our break.

'I love laughing too. It's good for the soul.'

"Oh, wow" she said chuckling while turning her head from side to side. "I'm not sure what it is, but it's even strange at this angle." Laughing even more as she stood at almost a 45 degree angle to the painting.

Her laughter was contagious and when she would start laughing the whole diner would be in a fit of laughter within minutes. Tuesdays and Thursdays were the most fun of the whole week.

"If I was to paint or draw something, I think I would like to be able to do a picture like this one." I said.

"Have you ever tried to draw or paint?" she asked.

"Not really, I tried once a long time ago when I was still in school, but I sat there the whole hour with just one line on the paper. I couldn't think of anything to draw. But you know something really weird came over me the first time I saw this painting. It really spaced me out a little, I was speechless and I felt like I had seen it before." I explained.

"I don't know about you, sometimes. You have a real strong imagination and you come in here sometimes saying the strangest things." she said shaking her head, laughing as she walked to the kitchen.

I could see that this was something I really had to wait and talk to Nell about. After all there are some things that you just can't talk to everyone about, but I was lucky.

Nell was one of those people that didn't judge anything a person said. She always said that a person was to be aloud their own ideas about things no matter how weird they sounded. Because only that person knew the whole thought behind their statement.

"Well, strange things happen when you have a great imagination like mine." I said laughing out loud.

We were both laughing now. After all it did sound funny, funny strange that is.

Drew was standing at the register as I turned around. "I love eating here on Tuesday. All of the laughter makes my day." He said with a big smile while putting tips in the jar.

The day went fast and it was time to go home. I knew Nell would be on her way home and I really wanted to talk to her. I hurried and put everything away and got ready to catch the bus.

"Hey Charlie, I have just enough time

for a soda before the bus comes. Okay?" I
yelled back to the kitchen.

Usually he'd tell me to go for it, but
there was no answer. *'Hum, he must be out
back. I guess I'll have a small one today. George
will be here soon; he comes in to get a coffee this
time of the day. He says it gets him though the
rush hour.'* I thought,

Sitting here with my soda and
looking at the painting, I feel like I'm being
pulled into it.

"Hey Rita. In deep thought? It's time
to go, I have my coffee and I need to get
these people to where they are going." said
George shaking my shoulder gently.

"What?" I said as I jumped back to the
present.

"Oh, hi, sure okay" I looked at my
soda and I hadn't even taken a drink.

"Okay Rita, You can bring it on the
bus this time. But don't spill It." he said.
"Rough day?" he questioned.

"No not really, every time I sit down

to really look at the new painting that Charlie bought, I get sucked into it. I'm not sure how to explain it." I said.

"Well, you have to agree, it is a real interesting painting. I mean changing like it does." he said. "I like it, don't get me wrong, but it's the first time I have ever seen anything like it." he added.

"It is out of the ordinary, I have to agree about that." I said as I we got on the bus.

Chapter 2

Then I spotted Nell at the back of the bus. She smiled and waved; I made my way back and sat down beside her.

"Wow, what a day," she said with a sigh.

"You too? So what happened to you today?" I asked.

"Well, let me think where to started." she said looking out the window then back at me. "Our law firm got a new client today and I had all this running around to do, people to see and things to do, you know."

My mind starting wondering and I was only able to catch part of what she was saying.

Then she stopped talking and that sort of brought me fully back to the here and now. I looked over at her and smiled.

"Okay, I can see that you have a lot on your mind, so ante up, what's happening?" she asked giggling softly.

"I'm sorry. I didn't mean to space out." I apologized.

"That's quite all right, but now you have to let me know what it is that's taking all of your attention." she said.

"It's that painting that Charlie brought back with him. I mean from the first time I saw it, I felt as if I was the one who painted it. There are times when I look at it and I have to look at my hands to make sure I'm not holding the paintbrush. I've tried to push it out of my mind, but I can't shake the feelings I get." I said trying to explain.

"Hum. That sounds strange. And I can only recall one other time I've heard of something like this but it was dealings with twins." she said looking closely at me.

"But I'm not a twin, at least not as far as I can remember my birth certificate saying. And my mom never mentioned it."

"When you get home tonight, take your birth record out and look at it." she suggested.

"Okay, but I can't see what one has to do with the other." I replied.

"Well, in some of the case studies I have read about twins. There are sometimes strong feelings between them. I mean what one does the other one can feel or knows about it. Sometimes it's like both of them are doing the same thing at the same time. Do you understand what I am saying?" she questioned, looking at me with a grin.

"I think so. Okay I will look at my birth record tonight and show it to you tomorrow." I said.

"I will look for those stories about twins. But meanwhile I want you to start writing down all of these thoughts and the time they happen and what was going on around you at the time.

There may be a correlation, a trigger that sets them off." she instructed. "I'll see you in the morning. This is your stop."

"Goodnight George I will see you in the morning." I yelled to the front of the bus.

"Night, have a good one, I'll see you in the morning." he said as I took the last step off the bus.

As I left the bus, Nell and I waved to each other.

Nell was the only one that I knew I could talk to without having to worry about being put in the loony been. She was like a safe haven for me.

Anna was sitting on the front steps, waiting for me as usual.

"Well, what have you been up to today?" I asked as I picked her up and took her upstairs with me.

Today is Anna's birthday and she is twelve years old. It's hard to believe that I have lived in this building for that long. Anna was born upstairs in 6B.

"Are you hungry girl?" I asked as I put her down.

Her bowl is the first place she always runs to.

"Okay hold on for a few minutes till I can get my sweater off." I said as I laid it over the couch, on my way to the kitchen. "There that's better."

I fed her, then headed for the living room to turn on the TV. She gobbled it down and looked eagerly for more.

My favorite programs were on this time of evening. It was my habit to feed my Anna, turn on the TV, relax a little, then make myself something for dinner, then let Anna have the leftovers, '*Yeah Right*'. She would sit on the arm of the chair and beg for part of my dinner and she knew she would get something.

Between the two of us, the plate was always empty before it got back to the kitchen. We usually get in the bed around ten o'clock.

But tonight, it looked like it could be a little different. As I was flipping through the TV channels a sci-fi program about time travel caught my attention. Time travel has always intrigued me.

Morning came fast, and when I woke up I found I had fallen asleep in the chair. All I remember is getting something to eat and sitting down to watch TV, and now waking up. I must have been more tired than I thought. I looked at the clock, *'good it's only 6:30, so I have enough time to find my birth records, get ready for work, eat and catch the bus.'*

Confused and a little disappointed I locked my door and put Anna on the front step as usual then hurried to catch the bus.

"Hi George" I said.

"You look down his morning." he said.

"Oh it's nothing. I just couldn't find

something I needed today." I explained.

"Well cheer up! You may find it when you get home this evening." he said.

"True." I said. I don't know why, but that made me feel a little better.

Then I saw Nell's smiling face, so I went and sat down beside her.

"So, what did the birth record say?" she asked.

"I couldn't find it. I thought I knew just where it was. But it wasn't there. I know I haven't moved it. It's always been in the top dresser drawer for the last twelve years, along with all my other important papers." I explained.

"Well don't be so down; you can always get another copy. After all I work close enough to the courthouse to pick up a copy while I'm downtown today, if you want me to?" she offered.

"Yes please, that will help relieve a lot of stress for me. Thank you." I said.

"So tell me, did anything strange

happen last night?" she asked.

"Now that you ask, yes, I feel asleep in the living room chair. I've never done that before. I remember watching a Sci-Fi about time travel while eating dinner. The next thing I remember was waking up this morning." I explained.

"Oh, not to worry, you may have just been more tired than you thought." she said.

"And another thing, you remember the new painting that Charlie bought for The Rooster?" I asked.

She nodded.

"Well, I am still getting those strange feelings when I see it. I still feel as if I am the one who painted it. I really don't understand it." I stressed.

"Well, things will become clearer as time goes by. They usually do." reassured Nell. "And I will get you a copy of your birth record while I'm on my lunch today."

"Thanks. Hopefully that will give me some answers. This is my stop. I'll see you on the way home." I said while getting off the bus.

Walking into the Rooster, I found that the place was almost packed.

"Looks like business is really good today." I said as I greeted Sandy.

"Right" she said smiling, "and tips are great."

She worked early mornings, from 5:00 a.m. till just after the lunch rush at 1:30pm. But as I looked around, I was beginning to wonder if there was a set time for rushes now.

The day went well, the cafe stayed full most of the day. It seemed that the news about the painting was getting around.

Later that afternoon Betty came to work, just in time to help set up for Dinner.

Motioning for me to follow her, "Come here, I want to show you something really strange," she said.

I followed her over to the new painting.

"See the signature of the artist," she said pointing at the artist name. "It looks like your signature."

We have worked together long enough for Betty to know my signature very well.

"Yes," I said, but when I looked at it closer, I started feeling very light headed and the next thing I knew I was coming to with a wet cloth on my forehead.

"What happened?" I asked.

"Well, you looked at the initials on the painting, and said "the same" and passed out...so you tell me," she said looking puzzled.

"I'm not sure what is going on. I wish I did know. The initials on this painting are the same as my middle and last name, and what is even stranger is that I sign them the same way.

All I know is every time I look at this painting, I feel like I am caught in a science fiction episode." I tried explaining, still feeling light headed and fuzzy.

"The signature is what I wanted you to see, but I didn't know that you would faint." said Betty motioning for Charlie.

Walking over to us, Charlie said, "I want you to take a few days off. You seem to be having problems since I brought in this painting.... any idea why?"

"No, it just seems strange to me. Like as if I have seen it before somewhere, and the artist's initials look a lot like mine." I explained while getting to my feet.

Taking off my hat and apron, I handed them to Betty. "I guess I will see you in a few days," I said as I grabbed my purse and book.

It was close to my regular quitting time anyway. So I sat down at the counter and drank a soda while waiting for the bus.

"I wish I knew what was going on. I really do...every time I look at that painting, I feel like I am caught in a science fiction episode," I said trying to explain things to

Charlie.

Looking at me, he just shook his head, "You've always been the strangest of my workers. But you are a good worker so I think I'll keep you." he said with a smile and laughing eyes.

"Your bus is here," Betty shouted from a front table.

"Okay, thanks," I replied while gathering my things.

"We will see you in a few days," said Charlie.

"Ok" I said as I walked out to catch my bus.

"Hi George, aren't you going in to get your coffee today?" I asked.

"No, we are running a little late, have to catch the clock," he said laughingly.

"How was your day?" he asked.

"Weird," I said, looking for Nell. "*Ah there you are,*" I thought.

I looked at George with a smile I said, "Better now that I 'm on my way home".

"Hi Nell," I shouted with a wave, walking toward our favorite place, at the back of the bus.

"So anything interesting happen today?" she asked.

"That's an understatement," I replied. "Oh? So tell me." she begged, almost bouncing in her seat.

So I told her all that had happened that day. By that time it was almost time to get off the bus.

"So, did you get a copy of my birth records?" I asked.

"Yes, here is what I found or I should say what was handed to me at the records office." she said handing it to me.

"It looks a little odd to me, but take it home and look it over." Taking a quick look out the window, she continued. "Tomorrow is Saturday and I thought you could come over and we can check things out together. What do you think?"

"That sounds good to me," I said, "I'll

call you in the morning. Here is my stop.

"See you later." I shouted to George. Waving as I got off the bus and giving a smile to Nell.

Gathering up Anna, we went upstairs to our apartment. I glanced over the mail and thought about what to fix for dinner. After cooking some macaroni and cheese with slices of hotdog, I sat down in my favorite chair to watch some TV. After about three hours of TV, I got ready to go the bed. I set my alarm so I could get a few things done before going to Nell's house.

I woke up about two minutes before my alarm and started my laundry and dishes.

"I'm feeling tired even though we went to bed fairly early last night." I told Anna.

She responded with a long meow and a big stretch as if to agree.

"Finally everything here at the house is caught up and the rest of the day is mine." I

thought.

Putting my birth record in my pocket, picked up my keys, gathered up Anna, locked my apartment door and we headed down stairs.

I placing Anna on the steps, "You be a good kitty today, I will be back in a while", I said petting her on the head.

Nell only lives about eight blocks from me, just a good walk on a nice day like today.

It seemed that a bird was singing in every tree along the way, lots of children having fun with their friends and pets. I couldn't help but be happy and smile the whole way.

I walked up Nell's steps and knocked on her door.

"Hi Rita, come on in, we have a lot to talk about," she said, while reaching past me to lock the screen door.

We headed down a long hallway to her kitchen.

"I feel a little tired this morning and my head feels full," I said as I sat down at the table.

"I just put on a pot of water a few minutes ago, it should be hot by now. Would you like a cup of tea?" she asked, walking toward the stove.

"Y yes, that sounds nice," I stuttered looking at my birth record.

Placing two cups of hot water on the table in front of us, "So, do you remember anything about last night?" she asked.

"Very little, I must have tossed and turned all night, because when I looked in the mirror this morning, I almost scared myself," I said with a chuckle.

"Do you remember any of your dreams from last night?" she inquired.

"Not really, just bits and pieces, and most of them seem real odd," I answered.

Chapter 3

She brought out a notebook and shoved it into my hand, "I want you to start writing down all your dreams, thoughts and feelings that you think may be connected to that painting at work." she said. "Here is a pen, get started, we have all-day and then some," she continued with a smile.

So I took the notebook and pen and stared to write, while she shared some of the studying she had been doing on the subject of twins.

"Did you have a chance to look at your birth record yet," she asked.

"Not yet, but I brought it with me," I replied.

Unfolding it, I could see that is was different from what I remembered. I couldn't put my finger on it, but something in my gut said it wasn't right.

"It doesn't look right to me, I'm not sure what it is though," I said.

"I thought the same thing when I collected it from the courthouse yesterday. So when I got home, I took mine out and took a long look at it. I couldn't quite place it either till you pulled it out just now," she said.

Placing her birth record on the table right beside mine, our eyes got wide, both our jaws dropped a little and I had chills run up my back and over my arms. "I think I know what the difference is." I almost shouted. "The paper is different, and the seal is a little off."

"I know, I can see that now, but till now I couldn't place what was wrong," she said, trembling with excitement.

"So what does this mean," I asked, sure she would have as answer.

"Well there is only one good reason I

can come up with right now, but I can't be sure about it," she said.

"Yes and what is that?" I asked on the edge of my seat.

"You say that you remember reading your birth records time and time again. And that you were a single birth?" she questioned.

"Yes," I answered.

"Well, look at it now," she pointed at my record.

"I-i-i it says I am a twin, how can that be, I have looked at my records so many times in the past and I was always an only child. How could it have changed? Maybe they got my name mixed up with someone else who has the same last name," I stuttered.

"No, if you look closer, you will see that all the rest of the information on this record belongs to you, your date and time, place, mother and father's name and even the address," she said pointing at the paper I now held in my hands.

"Yes, I see that, but how? How could this be? I inquired.

"Well, I am pretty sure that someone has been tampering with your records. That seems pretty clear to me," she explained. "So you need to keep a good record in that notebook so we can solve this mystery." she added.

As I began to write, the pages filled up quickly. When I looked up from my writings it was almost noon and Nell was fixing us some sandwiches.

While we ate lunch, she read what I had written so far.

"Some of these things could be considered weird but I think there may be a good reason for all of them and we will find out what that is and the sooner the better," she said with a smile.

She was like me in that way, we both liked mysteries and puzzles. Every once in a while, when we both had the same Saturday off, we would watch a mystery movie and tell each other who we thought did it, before the end.

"You know Rita, I think that it may be a good idea to go ask Charlie, your boss, where he got that painting." Nell suggested.

"How about if we both go find out right now, I mean after lunch?" I said.

"Great idea, how I do love a good mystery." she said with a laugh.

We hurried though lunch. Got the dishes done and almost ran to the bus stop. We were so energized and excited by the whole idea of solving a mystery for real that we had almost forgotten that it was my life we were solving.

"Hi George." we said together.

"Oh hi Rita, hi Nell, I thought you two would be watching a mystery," he said.

"We are, sort of." Nell laughed.

"Huh?" he questioned.

"We are on a case today since I'm off for the next few days." I answered.

"Yeah, we have our own mystery to solve," we said together with a giggle as we hurried to the back of the bus.

Sitting down in our usual place, Nell asked, "You know Rita, I'm just curious, but if you could have picked your own name? What name would you have picked to be called?"

"Oh I don't know, I was always fond

of Anna Marie Stolks, I guess that is why I named my cat Anna. Why?"

"Well according to all the info I have studied on twins, most of them like the same things, and do most things in the same way. Some of them even think the same thoughts or at least know what is happening in the other one's life at times. That is one reason I want you to start keeping record of the things that you think are sort weird or at least strange in your life and also your dreams." she explained.

"Ok, I think I can do that, I have the notebook with me, see?" I said, holding it up.

"Good, something that you may not have thought of or connected to this whole thing..." her voice trailed off.

"What?" I asked.

"Is it just the signature on the painting, or what made you think it so strange?" she asked with a straight face.

"Well, it was signed A.M.S. and it

looks like I was the one that signed it, I mean the M and S look just the way I make them."

"Well, if we are going to solve this mystery then that is the kind of things you need to keep track of, so write that down, along with the time a date that you discovered it." she suggested.

I opened the notebook and began to write it all down.

"Here we are, our stop is the next one." she said nudging me.

I hurried as fast as I could to get it all written down before having to get off the bus. I closed the notebook just as the bus came to a stop and the doors opened.

We said goodbye to George almost in unison and got off the bus just as a light shower started, we pulled our jackets a little closer around us and hurried a little faster. But before we got to the door of The Rooster it started to really pour. We were drenched by the time we made it through the doors and we stood there dripping for a few minutes.

Fred peered over the warming tray and started to laugh. I thought he would start rolling on the floor any minute.

"It's not that funny," I said.

Then turning to look at Nell, I started to laugh, then I caught sight of a reflection of myself in the window, and really busted out laughing. By this time Nell had figured it out too and joined in the laughter.

Somehow our hair was standing up on end, and her makeup was running, we were a funny sight ok. After a few minutes of laughter we all settled down.

"Hey Fred, where is Charlie?" I asked.

Fred is a short and stocky sort, always looking for the up side to everything. He's always telling a funny story, if not about himself, it was one he had heard somewhere. On slow days at work, he would keep us laughing. He said laughter was better for a person than food.

"He'll be back in a bit, he just went to the bank." came the answer.

"Ok, well, I'm grabbing me and Nell a couple of sodas while we wait." I informed Fred, who was in the back part of the kitchen, as Betty came walking through the half doors leaving them swinging behind her.

"Fine by me," he said still chuckling.

Using some of the paper-towels behind the counter, we wiped off our faces and slicked our hair back. While sipping on our sodas, we decided to go and have a closer look at the painting again.

"Fred?" questioned Nell. "I thought he was Charlie."

"No that's Fred our fry cook," I explained as we walked over to the painting.

"You see, right there they are. The A.M.S. and the MS is just the way I make them." I said.

I have to agree, they do look real close to the way you sign them." Nell said, squinting to look at them closer.

"Oh Nell, don't tell me, you left your reading glasses on the table?" I joked.

"Ok, I won't tell you," she laughed. "Can I borrow yours'?"

"Sure, here." I said taking mine out of my pocket and handing them to her.

Putting them on, she looked at the signature, her eyes grew large. "Wow, I see what you mean now, it does look like you signed the painting." she exclaimed.

"That is what just added to the strangeness of this whole thing." I said.

"Hey Charlie, Rita is waiting for you over next to the painting." Fred announced.

"Yes, I see her, thanks Fred."

As I turned to see him, he was walking to the back of the cafe.

"Charlie!" I waved.

"Be with you in a minute," he said, opening the door to his office.

"Rita," Nell said touching me on the shoulder. "We want to get as much information as he can give us on this painting," she said in almost a whispering tone.

"I know, I have a lot of question for him." I said.

"Ok Rita, come join me over here," he said pouring himself a cup of coffee and motioning to a corner booth.

Nell and I took our sodas and joined him in the booth.

"Ok, tell me why you are here and not taking the day off," he said with a grin.

"I can't shake the feelings I'm having and have had since you brought this painting to the Rooster." I replied.

"And what are they?" he inquired.

"That I have seen it before or somehow I'm connected with it." I tried explaining.

"What can you tell us about it?" I asked.

"Not that much, I don't think, but I will try." he said.

"Well first, where did you get it? What was the artist name? How much did you pay for it. What history did you find out about it when you bought it?" asked Nell.

"Humm, well to start, I bought it for $380 from a small shop on West Slome street in Queens. Mr. Yauny, the owner, said that this lady came in one day and wanted to know if she could sell her work on consignment. He said yes and so he did. He didn't tell me anything other than that about the painting." Charlie explained.

"Well, I guess that is a start. On Slome St you say?" Nell questioned.

"Yes 358 West Slome St., it's a small shop, sort of a hole in the wall place." he explained.

"So how did you know about it?" I asked.

"I grew up in the neighborhood and Mr. Yauny always had candy for us kids and little jobs for us to do. He's a good old man. I went to visit him the other day like I do once in a while and I happen to tell him I was looking for something special to put in my cafe that would help to bring in customers. He laughed and said he had just the thing. He took me down stairs in his shop and showed me the painting, saying it had just come in the night before. "Sort of magical" he says, "things like this only come into my shop if someone is coming for them soon" he continued. So he took it in on consignment. Don't know anything else." Charlie said.

"All of that helps a lot." I said, encouraged.

"We need to hurry if we are going to catch George on his way through this time," nudged Nell.

While getting up, I thanked Charlie.

"So why all the questions?" he asked.

"It's a mystery for right now, we can let you know more later." Nell interjected.

"I have an idea." Nell said looking at me strangely.

"What?" I asked, wondering what she

was up to now.

"Follow me." she said walking into Billy's Drugs and Varity store next door.

I followed to find out what she had in mind. We ended up trying out some of the makeup samples that Nell put on me. Then she backed up a little and looked at me. "I always wondered what you would look like with makeup on." she said with a big smile. "Look." she said. "You are something else with it on." she added.

"I look different somehow." I said looking in the mirror hanging nearby.

We waved and ran out the door to flag down George.

"Boy! You two are really cutting it short today. I almost didn't see you in time to stop," he laughed.

"We're glad you did, we are putting a puzzle, a mystery together. How close do you come to West Slome St.? I inquired.

"Oh not too far, if you don't mind the walk, it's about a half mile west of my last stop on this run." he informed us.

"Ok, that is where we are going," said Nell.

"So tell me more," he quizzed.

"Not yet, wait till we can tell you the whole story," I said.

"Well, Ok if I must," he said like a small child on Christmas.

We sat down right behind him for this trip. While watching the buildings move swiftly past the window, we talked, laughed and watched the bus become almost empty.

"Ok girls, this is your stop," George announced as he turned to look at us. With a smile he continued, "hope you solve your mystery. The street you asked about is right down this street about six or seven blocks."

Thanking George, we got off the bus and waved goodbye. "See you in about two hours if all goes well." I said, waving again.

"I go home in three, so hurry, I want in on your mystery." he said with a chuckle.

Walking as fast as we could, we were

finally in the right area. "Here is West Slome St.: I announced.

"And this is the 300 block...oh look there is 346, so it must be on our side of the street." add Nell.

The area was mixed with brownstone apartment houses and small family businesses. "Here it is." I said pointing at a small store.

It looked small from the outside and unimportant. There was only a simple signs in the window that said "Yauny's Specialty shop". But, when we walked into the shop,

"WOW!" I exclaimed. "I would have never thought this place would be this large from the outside. Art work, paintings and collectables went way back on either side making a larger path in the center and smaller ones dividing different areas."

The shop was very deep. We found out later that there was even an upstairs and downstairs to the shop.

"Hello Ladies, anything I can help

you with?" We were shocked back to the present by a kind sounding voice from behind us.

Then, when I turned around, his eyes widened and his mouth slightly open, "I remember you, I think...or it is someone that looks a lot like you." he said sort of smoothing his hair. "Old age you know, sometimes plays tricks on me...of course, you are you and the other is some else and not the same, I can see that now looking more closely at you."

Mr. Yauny was a short small man with white hair and mustache. He had such a pleasant manner it was like talking to an old friend.

"My boss, Charlie, came in a few days ago and bought a painting from you." I blurted.

"Oh yes, Little Charlie, well not so little now I guess, but I've known him all his life. He used to come and sweep for me once in a while. Good guy." he said smiling.

"Yes, well, we want to know more about that painting that he got from you." interjected Nell

"Well, there's not much to tell. The lady, she looks a lot like you." he said pointing at me.

"And?" urged Nell.

"Well, uh, let me think." he said playing with his mustache. "Oh yes, she asked if I could sell her painting for her on consignment and I told her yes, and so she left it here and walked out. Saying she'd be back and that's all I can remember right off hand." he said, looking straight at me. "You know, you really look a lot like her." he added.

"Did you have her sign something?" questioned Nell, "You know something to show she left the painting?"

"No, I was getting the paperwork ready when she walked out of the shop, but she did say her name was Anna May something." he said looking toward the ceiling.

Chapter 4

"Anna May Stolks?" I asked.

"Yes! I think that was the name she said." he said with a slight smile.

"And did she happen to mention where you could find her" I asked.

"No, not really, but I did notice that she used a special paint in some parts of the painting," he said. "And if memory serves me right today, there is only one place she could get it as far as I know." he added.

"Where, where?" Nell jumped in.

"Let me look it up," he said walking slowly toward the back of his shop.

Upon arriving at his desk, he started fumbling through some papers piled on it. Stopping, he stroked his hair back and said, "No, it's not there, now where did I put that paper?" he said aloud, talking to himself. "Oh, yes, it is in my top drawer." he said shuffling through more papers and then through a stack of business cards. "AH! HA!, Here it is!" he said proudly holding up a card. "I will write this information down for you," he said looking around for a pencil.

Nell grabbed a pen from her pocket and almost shoved it at him, and said. "Here use mine."

"Oh, aren't you a dear," he replied reaching for the pen. He read off the information as he wrote it down, the said "This shop belongs to a friend of mine. Her name is Lucinda Mains and the name of her shop is "Magical Arts for the Artist" as he handed the pen and paper to Nell, who already had her hand out.

"1372 Blane Street is about three blocks down this street and just around the corner from here." he explained. "She may have more information for you." he added with a smile.

"Thank you," said Nell.

"Yes, thank you, but can you do one more thing for me?" I asked.

"And what would that be my dear?" he asked looking over at me.

"Well, when Anna May comes back in about her painting, can you ask her to come to "The Rooster Cafe'?" I asked with a smile.

"Sure, that will not be a problem." he said with a warm smile.

"Thanks again, we will see you again," I said with a small wave as Nell grabbed me by the arm and we walked back to the front of the shop and out the door.

"Nell, do we have time to go over to Blane Street and still catch George on his last run?" I asked

Looking at her watch and thinking for a few seconds, "We have 2 hours and ten minutes. So what do you think?" she asked with a grin.

"Well, if we figure it will take us thirty minutes to get back to where we have to meet George, then we won't have to run to catch the bus. Yeah, let's do it but make it sort of fast." I said as we started walking in the direction of Blane Street.

On the way I spotted a pet shop and in the window was a cozy cat bed, "Oh look Nell, I've been looking for one of those for Anna" I said, and we both started laughing. "I mean **My** Anna." I added.

Grabbing me by my sleeve, Nell said "we don't have time for Cat Beds today if we are going to solve this mystery."

"Oh yeah," I said with a sigh and a slight chuckle as she pulled me away from the window.

"Blane Street should be at this next light," Nell informed me.

"Which way do we go, when we get there? Any idea?" I asked.

"No, we still have to look for addresses like we did before, she laughed.

"Oh, I see 1401 over the door of the building across the street." I said pointing.

"Then 1372 should be in this direction and on our side of the street." she said laughing. "This is fun, a real mystery and it's ours to solve." she added.

"Here it is!" I said pointing at the address on the bottom of the door under the mail slot.

A little bell hanging over the door rang as Nell opened it and again as I closed it.

"Hello, and what can I help you with today?" asked a voice from somewhere near the back of the shop.

Paintings hung on the walls show ways to use certain paints, while others showed different techniques of creating special effects.

"We have a few questions we need the answers to." said Nell in almost a shout.

I was busy looking around while we waited on the lady to come and talk to us.

A round smiling face with a wide floppy brimmed hat soon peered around some books on a desk from the back of the shop. "I'll be with you in a moment," she said.

In a short time, this sort of plump little woman, that looked to be in her late 60's came walking up the narrow isle of the shop toward us.

Wiping her hands on an old apron hanging from her waist, "Hi my name is Lucinda but most people just call me Lou." she said reaching out to shake hands with Nell.

"Hi Lou, my name is Nell and this is my friend Rita." she said as I turned around to meet her.

Lou put on her glasses that had been hanging around her neck from a chain, "You mean Anna don't you?" she said looking at me and Nell.

"No, this is Rita, we are here about Anna," said Nell. "What can you tell us about her?" she asked.

"Not much, I'm afraid. Are you kin to her?" Lou asked looking at me.

"We're not sure yet." Nell answered quickly. "That is what we want to find out." she added.

"Well, I remember her saying something about the Clair Mont, now I don't know if that is where she is staying or if it was somewhere close to there." she said, "But I think you must be kin and real close, because the two of you just look too much alike not to be." she added, looking through her glasses at me again with a smile. "And that's about it except that she paid cash for all of the supplies she bought, a little over $400 worth, if memory is working today, that was a little over three weeks ago now. Sorry I couldn't help more." she said.

"I think you may have helped, at least it gives us a little more information than when we walked in. But just in case she comes back, can you ask here to call me?"

Nell asked, quickly writing down her phone number and handing it to Lou.

"Not a problem," she said shoving the paper into her vest pocket.

We waved and said, "Goodbye". As we hurried out the door and back the way that we had come so we could get to the bus stop before George.

When we came around the corner where we were to meet George, we noticed the bus. "Look! There's the bus. Oh, man the light is red. I hope he waits," I said.

"GEORGE!" yelled Nell. George stuck his head out his side window to see who was calling his name.

"Well, it's about time you two showed up. I've been here waiting for about 10 minutes," he said with a laugh.

Looking at her watch, Nell said, "but you are ahead of schedule."

"I know, I was in a hurry to hear what you two were doing, I mean this mystery and all." George said with a large grin as we stepped up onto the bus. "I didn't notice earlier. But Rita, you look different. I can't put my finger on it. But there is a difference." He added, looking closer at Rita.

"Oh, I wanted to see what I would look like with makeup on. Nell helped. We got it all at the drugstore next to The Rooster after I talked to Charlie this morning.

We sat up in front with him on the way back long enough to tell him everything that had happened so far since Charlie had brought the painting to The Rooster Cafe.

Three stops into the route, others started getting on the bus.

"I want to know as soon as you find out more," he said, "I love mysteries as well as you two. Promise?" he requested.

"Sure we will. It's not like we will be going to check on anything without you taking us, now is it?" asked Nell and we all laughed.

"No, I g   not." he replied and

with that we   ed to our favorite seats in

the back of   us.

        "N   re we going to check out the

Clair M   omorrow?" I asked.

         at sounds like it could be fun.

Yes. C e over to my house in the

mor g." she said.

        "Ok, that's a deal. I'll meet you at

y   house. Shall we eat a little something,

e we did today." I asked.

        "Sure sounds good to me." she said.

        "Ok, I'll see you then. This is my

stop, see you tomorrow." I said while going

for the door. "Bye George" I said getting off

the bus and giving Nell a wave as they

drove away.

        Anna, my cat, stood up from the

wide banister where she had been laying

and stretched when she spotted me walking

toward our apartment building. She jumped

down to greet me and rubbed against my

legs meowed loudly.

"Are you hungry?" I asked picking her up and carrying her upstairs to our apartment.

I sat her down on the couch on my way to the bedroom. "Were you a good girl today?" I asked Anna while changing my clothes.

She jumped off the couch and came running into the bedroom and jumped onto the bed. Standing up straight and tall, she meowed a few more times before lying down. Then she rolled over onto her back and waved her paws around in the air and meows some more..

"Well, come on, let's go get dinner started." I said heading for the kitchen while flipping on the TV on my way through the living room.

Anna had jumped off the bed and was right on my heels. "Now don't get stepped on, I know you're hungry, you already told me that." I said stooping over to stroke her back. "Now go lie down, and I will have dinner ready for both of us in a few minutes." I explained.

Anna trotted off towards the living room and bounced onto the couch and curled up facing the TV.

I had just turned on the oven for our two TV dinners when the TV announced the move for tonight. It was to be another time travel movie, *"that sounds interesting, so I had better hurry and get dinner on the way,"* I thought.

Hearing a can being opened, Anna cocked her ears, and immediately jumped off the couch and headed for the kitchen.

"Yes, I know you hear me opening a can, but you do need to remember that all cans that are opened aren't just for you. Sometimes I open a can for me." I said with a smile. "But this one is for you." I said lifting the lid of the can.

She meowed with joy and followed the can from the cabinet to her bowl in the corner near the stove. Pouring most of it into her bowl I give her a pat on the head, "Now be careful the oven in hot." I said, "I'm putting in two TV dinners for us tonight, so we will both have enough to eat." I added.

She seemed to understand what I was saying as she looked up at me and meowed and moved her tail over a little.

Just then the TV caught my attention again. The Sci-Fi was getting ready to start.

"When you are finished, you can come and join me on the couch." I said looking back over at Anna. "I am going to watch a little TV while our dinners are heating up." I explained.

What seemed like just a few minutes pasted when, "Meow! MEOW!!" she said almost as if she was yelling at me.

"You're so loud, I can't hear the TV," I said getting up to see what she was talking about. "OH MY! Good Girl! You saved our dinners. You know I think that someday you may be able to cook." I said with a chuckle while taking our dinners out of the oven.

Placing them on the counter I turned off the oven, then I reached over and gave her a stroke on her back.

I took our dinners into the living room with me and put them on my TV tray next to the couch. Then reaching for Anna's TV tray, which was under the couch, I placed it on the couch beside Anna and me. I knew if I didn't put her tray there that she would be in my face wanting a bite of my dinner. I cut up the meat into bite size pieces and placed a few on her tray while I ate some of my dinner and watched more of the Time Travel movie that was on TV.

After we ate I took both trays to the kitchen during a commercial, then sat back and watched the rest of movie while petting Anna.

The movie was about a guy that went back in time to help himself, but he knew that if he was to touch his other self that it would destroy both of them.

After the movie was over we watched the news and then went to bed.

The sun peering through my window and the neighborhood dogs barking at the garbage truck, woke me up and of course as soon as I moved Anna was in my face meowing for breakfast.

Chapter 5

"Anna, you would not believe the dream I had last night, "I said sitting up and putting on my slippers. "Breakfast will be ready in a moment." I continued while turning slightly to pet her. She was now doing her cat stretches at the foot of the bed.

By the time I got to the kitchen, she was there rubbing up against the cabinets and meowing. "I know, I know, you are sure spoiled, aren't you Anna?" I asked while opening the fridge and getting out the milk. "Yeah, I think they have this bit all turned around, when they say people train animals, because I think you guys train us." I said while petting her with a slight chuckle. I wish I knew what you do all day while I'm at work. I bet you hang out on the roof or in the tree and watch people or go hunting at Mr. Berealy's market for meat scraps or just sleep, don't you pretty girl?"

"Well, enough of this, I have to fix the rest of your breakfast, get me something to eat, wash the dishes and straighten up the kitchen. Then I need to straighten up the house, get dressed and take out the garbage before it is time to meet with Nell and you get to play outside today." I said as Anna finished her milk.

We finished eating and I did my chores while Anna played with her toy mouse. She came running into the bedroom meowing, jumped up onto the end of the bed and paced back and forth while I brushed my hair

"Anna, we will leave your toy right where it is for right now. I am ready to leave the house and go to Nell's." I said after putting down the hairbrush. "Your toy will be there waiting on you later today when we get home." I explained while grabbing my jacket with my free hand before locking the door.

"Now you be a good girl today and stay safe." I said placing her on the bottom step and giving her a few strokes. Then I went down the street towards Nell's house.

On the way there, I found a five-dollar bill wadded up against the light post. *"What a find."* I thought while stuffing it into my jean pocket. I decided since I wasn't working today I was going to wear my comfortable but nice clothes like my blue jeans, the peasant blouse with my flats since I figured we would be doing a lot of walking and standing. After all, we were going to check out the Clair Mont today.

Knocking on Nell's door, I remembered the dream I had last night.

"Oh. Hi Rita, I slept late. I was just putting on my makeup when you knocked on the door, Come on in, I will only be a few minutes." she said opening the screen door for me.

I followed her to the bathroom, hoping to tell her about the dream I had, but instead we talked about ways to check out the Clair Mont and finding other clues while she finished her makeup. Then she put some on me. Then we went to the kitchen for some juice.

"I had a wild dream last night but thinking about it, the movie I watched might have had something to do with it." I said while Nell made us some toast. "Only one for me, I ate at home." I said holding up one hand.

"So tell me about it." she said sitting down with a plate of ham and cheese, so we could have sandwiches. "I will put these together for lunch later." she added.

"I only remember the main part, I know there was more but I guess one only remembers the important things in a dream," I said.

"That sounds about right. So out with the dream, already," she said with a giggle.

"Ok, well somehow I was at work and I guess it was Anna that walked in and sat down at a table. Somehow I guess, Charlie thought it was me. He went over and asked if I thought it was break time and for me to get back to work. Well Anna just looked at him and started laughing and said "I guess some things stay the same."

I was standing behind the counter at this point and Anna pointed at me and laughed even harder.

"Are you twins?" Charlie asked her and she said "Maybe, or maybe we are sisters sort of," and he wanted to know what she meant and he sat down and talked to her. I didn't get a chance to hear what was being said.

"Oh man! That would have been the best part." interrupted Nell. "So was that the end of the dream?"

"Yeah pretty much, I got called into the kitchen and when I came out she and

Charlie were gone." I said.

"Did you right this one down in your log?" Nell questioned.

"Not yet. I just remembered it on the way here." I said.

"Maybe do that while on the bus ride to the Clair Mont." suggested Nell. "So are you ready to check out the Clair Mont?" she asked looking at the clock, "because George will be by in about ten minutes." she added while bagging our sandwiches.

"The wind was blowing and the clouds were moving in on my way here." I said.

"Then we had better take my umbrella." she said grabbing it as we hurried through the door and she closing it tight behind us.

"Hurry! I see the bus now." I said motioning for her to hurry.

Hurrying to catch the bus in almost a run, I waved George down and he stopped even though we were between stops.

"Ok Girls, Hurry up! And get on the bus, this isn't a regular stop you know." he said laughing as we panted.

"Thanks for stopping George. We almost got to the stop before you did." I said laughing after catching my breath.

"Where are you two going today in such a hurry?" he asked.

Nell and I looked at each other and laughed. "Well…"Nell said, "We are off to gather more clues in our mystery." Then looked at me again as we all laughed.

"Now remember you said you would keep me up on it." He reminded us with a chuckle. "So where are you headed today?"

"We are going to check out the Clair Mont today. We heard that Anna was staying somewhere in the area." said Nell with a grin.

"Then you gals will need these," he said pushing two transfers into Nell's hand.

"Okay." I said taking one, "So where do we get off and what do we need to catch?" I asked, looking at him over the top of the transfer in my hand.

"You will need to get off at the end of my route and then take the Monte St bus east about 12 blocks, then you will need to walk north about 4 blocks to the Clair Mont." he explained

"So how come you know where it is and which way to go?" I asked.

"I have a brother that comes to visit once in a while and that is where he stays. It is real nice." he answered. "Anna is lucky if that is where she is staying." he added.

"Ok. Well, let us know when we get there, we will be in our usual seats." said Nell as we walked toward the back of the bus.

Sitting down on a seat in the back, Nell took out a piece of paper and started writing something down.

"What are you writing?" I asked.

"The direction that George just gave us, I figure this way if we get side tracked or excited about something, we won't have to try and remember our way home." she explained.

"Good idea." I agreed.

"And you need to write down your dream." Nell reminded me.

Thanks, I'd forgotten about that." I said while taking out my notebook and a pen.

Then we just sat back and enjoyed the rest of the ride.

We were watching the people on the streets, holding on to their coats, hats and whatever packages they happened to have. The wind looked like it was picking up, and it made me glad I had brought my jacket.

"Ok, this is where you have to get off and you go across the street over there and catch the other bus." George said pointing across the street at a bench that had bus stop written on it. "Now remember, I leave here on my last run back at 6pm tonight. So if you want to ride back home with me you will have to be here and this time be on time, OK?" he added questioning our timing.

"Ok, got it, that gives us a little over 5 and half-hours to take care of all that we need to do." said Nell looking at her watch as we smiled at each other.

"Bye girls" said George with a wave as we got off the bus, "And Good Luck" he added.

"Well according to this sign, we have about 20 minutes before the bus gets here." Nell said looking at the bus schedule posted on the bench.

While sitting there the wind started picking up again. We drew our jackets a little tighter around our shoulders and sat closer together, the wind continued to get colder with a light mist mixed in.

"I hope it doesn't keep this up for very long, I'm starting to get colder." said Nell.

Looking up I saw the bus, "Here

comes the bus now and it will give us the break from the weather that we need." I informed Nell.

"But then we have that last 4 blocks to walk in this." she said.

"Well maybe by then it will let up," I said hoping I would be right.

"Hello, we want to get off as close as we can to the Clair Mont." Nell told the bus driver as we got on the bus and handed her our transfers.

"Oh you got off George's bus." she said looking closely at both of us, "and will you be coming back this way later this evening?" she questioned.

"Yes, George said we had to be back here by 6pm in order to catch him." I told her.

"Well in order to do that you will have to catch me at 5:10 pm across from where I drop you off. That way you will get here in time to catch George." she informed us. "Sit up here close so I can let you know where to get off." she added.

We sat down in the seats right across from her and watched the streets fly by, it turned out that we were on an express bus! We found out later that they only hit the main stops on their way through.

"Ok, here is where you get off and over there is where you need to be at 5:10pm." She said pointing across the street at a post with a schedule posted on it.

"Thanks" we said almost in unison as we got off the bus.

Chapter Six

"Well that was nice of her to let us know when to be here on our way back," said Nell.

"Yeah, I think she knows George." I said looking around for memorable markers, so I would know where we needed to be later to catch the bus back.

Nell was already writing down the cross streets and the address near the stop. "There now we will know just where to be when we get back here." she said putting her notebooks and pen back into the vest pocket of her jacket.

"I think that the Clair Mont is this way" I said pointing up the street.

"Me too," Nell said as we started walking.

About that time the wind started picking up again. Walking faster we tried to out run the rain, we only had one block to go. It was misting as we got to the steps and just as we got to the doors of the Clair Mont, it was as if the bottom fell out of the cloud.

"Wow, just in time." I said taking a deep breath. "I think if we had opened your umbrella the wind would have turned it wrong side out." I added.

"You're telling me, and look at it come down, boy I'm glad we're not out there now." Nell said with a great breath of relief.

Nell and I walked through the second doors of the Clair Mont and our jaws dropped.

"Wow! Will you look at this place?" Nell whispered motioning with her head toward the very large chandler that was hanging in the center of this extraordinarily lavish sitting room.

One of the bell hops came hurrying

toward us. "Anna, I am so glad you haven't left yet, I went by that café called The Rooster on my days off and got a chance to see your painting. Wow, that is so great." he said reaching out and grabbing my hand. "I just want to shake the hand of a great artist" he continued.

"I'm Rita not Anna." I interrupted and slowly withdrew my hand.

"But, you look so much like her." he said looking closely at me, with his mouth a gape.

"This is her sister Rita," Nell said jumping into the conversation quickly.

Looking over at Nell with what must have been a puzzled look on my face; she looked back at me and gave me a quick wink.

"So where is Anna anyway?" Nell asked, looking back at the bell hop.

"Oh sorry, my name is Nell and as you know now this is Rita," she said pulling her hand out of her pocket.

Shaking hands, "My name is Daniel James, but most people just call me Danny," he said with a pleasant smile, then reached over and shook my hand too.

He was a pleasant looking young man, about 6-foot tall with sandy red hair and blue eyes. He spoke in an energetic manner but with a peace and calmness at the same time.

"Rita works at the Rooster Cafe." Nell said getting Danny's attention off me. "So what time is Anna due back?" she asked.

"I'm not sure. The last time I saw her was before my days off and she said something about going on a trip to get inspiration for her next project. I think she is planning on painting another picture." he said, "But she didn't tell me where she was going." he added.

"So, is there a way to find out?" asked Nell. "We would like to see her before she goes back home."

"Wait right here and I will go see what I can find out." he said pointing to the spot where we were standing, as he hurried off in the direction of the hotel desk.

We could see him talking animatedly but couldn't hear what was being said.

Within a few minutes he came hurrying toward us again, so excited that he started talking before he got to us.

"Danny! Stop. Slowdown and start over, we missed the whole first part of what you were telling us." Nell, said holding up one hand. "Now tell us what you found out." she continued.

"Well, I found out that she has gone to France for about a week and then she will be in Spain for three days before coming back here." he said. "So we all just missed her. She left about 8 am this morning." he added.

Nell asked looking straight at Danny. "While I'm thinking of it, does Anna have any one here that she talks to a lot or that knows what she's been up to for the last few years?"

"It's just that it's been a while since I've seen or got a chance to talk to Anna." I added quickly. "Between her moving and me moving we lost contact for about the last three or so years."

"Oh I know what that's like. I have two brothers in my family that lost track of each other, or maybe they didn't want to talk, but they finally caught up with each other about a year ago. I think I might know someone." he said. "Anna has visited with me a lot of time, but there is one other person that she visited with even more than me, and that's Mandy, she is one of the house maids for the 2nd floor. She is about your height, er-uh, maybe a little shorter than you." he said while looking over at me. "She has very long black hair and usually has it tied back in a bun or a braid." he added.

"Since you have had a chance to visit

with her as you say, has she ever told you how she learned to paint?" I asked. "Because when we were growing up neither one of us could draw a straight line as they say." I added with a soft laugh.

"No, she has said that she had always wanted to be an artist, and by the looks of the painting that's hanging in the cafe, where you work, I would say that she has learned very well." he said with a pleased smile. "Talking about Mandy, she's coming this way."

"Hi Danny, are you on your lunch break?" she asked.

"No, just a slow morning." he answered

"Miss Anna! I thought you had already left on your trip," she said as our eyes met.

"No Mandy, this is Rita, Anna's sister. She works at the cafe' where Anna's painting is hanging." Danny explained.

"Glad to meet you Ms. Rita." said

Mandy with a slight curtsy.

While shaking hands with her, I asked, "Do you know Anna well?"

"I guess you can say pretty well, why?" she asked.

"Well, I haven't seen her for a very long time, and when the painting came into The Rooster Cafe, somehow I knew she must have been the one that painted it. I felt a connection to it." I explained trying not to sound to off the wall.

"Oh, well of course you did," she said. "Twins have that connection, and it is even hard for science to explain why, but they do. I think you two must be twins, you look so much alike. Except Anna's hair and eyebrows are a little lighter than yours." she said.

"Really? I always wondered what I would look like with lighter hair, maybe I will get the chance to find out." I said with a giggle.

"Did she ever tell you how she

learned to paint?" I continued.

"Yeah, matter of fact she did one time and I remember thinking it sounded very odd." she said, as her voice trailed off into thought.

"Odd in what way." asked Nell.

"Yeah, tells us." prodded Danny.

"Ok, Ok," she said, pushing Danny in the arm. "She told me that on one of her many travels, she ran across a great artist from India that said he could teach her to paint like the great painters of history. So she studied under him for several months, then he told her she was a master artist and sent her back to America. A few months later she was painting the painting that is hanging in The Rooster Cafe'."

"Wow! Now that's a story," said Nell. "And she learned to paint like that in a few months? I have known people that have studied painting all their lives and they can't paint a cat as well as a first grader." she continued with a chuckle.

"Well that is what she told me a few weeks ago when she had finished the painting." said Mandy. "It was nice to meet you Rita and you too" she said reaching out to shake hands with Nell.

'Nell, my name is Nell," she said shaking hands with Mandy.

"Sorry about that, Nell, I don't know what happened to my manners." apologized Danny.

"It's ok, it all came out alright, but I really need to eat while I have a chance." said Mandy.

"I just have one other question, if you don't mind." I said, looking at Mandy.

"Ok, but please make it a quick one." said Mandy.

Well, I was just wondering how long Anna had been staying here at the Clair Mont?" I asked.

Chapter Seven

"Well, let me see." she said trying to give us the most correct information as possible. "I have known her for the last 6 months but I think she lived on the 4th floor for a while before I met her. I'm going to lunch. See you later Danny." Mandy smiled as she walked off.

"Thanks Mandy!" I said before she got out of ear shot.

She waved and kept walking. Hearing a bell ring, I turned and looked at Danny, with a smile.

"Well, that's my Q, got to go, see you around." he said with a wave as he hurried away.

"So there you have it," said Nell, looking at me with a grin. "Are you ready to go back and catch our busses home?" she asked.

"Yeah, but first, let's take a short stroll through the garden since the weather seems to be clearing up." I suggested.

"Okay," Nell agreed.

The weeks flew passed and then it happened, just like in my dream.

After putting some plates away behind the counter at The Rooster, I stood up just in time to see Anna walk to the booth across from her painting and sit down. She was even wearing my favorite colors. She had on a peacock blue knitted sweater with jewels around the neck and tan suede looking slacks. She had her honey blonde hair in a French braid with a colorful bow in the end. She looked just like someone I would have wanted to be, if I had caught a break. But instead I was living my life just trying to meet my monthly bills, which never seemed to get caught up. Glancing in the mirror across the back of the cafe, I could see myself standing there with my mouth open slightly. My dish water brown hair had started to string down in my eyes and it was just noon. No need to wear makeup at work. It would be a mess within the first few trips into the kitchen. Yes there I was, standing there wiping my hands on my almost white apron which was stained in a way that looked like a great painter's master piece. I was wearing a uniform that had been crisp red and white once upon a time. *'Yep, here I am ok, and over there is what I would have liked to have been.'*

"Rita, Rita!, your order is up, came the voice from the kitchen, drawing me back to what was my reality. Charlie was talking to Anna and she was laughing as I headed to grab the order that had just come up. *'It was just like in my dream. I wonder if it will turns out the same.'* I thought.

Coming out of the kitchen with the whole order put together, I could see that the table where Anna was sitting was empty and Charlie wasn't anywhere to be seen either. *'Wow! Too much'*, I thought.

Going home that evening the day kept running through my head. "Hi, George." I said getting on the bus.

"You looking like you have had a very thoughtful day, Rita." said George touching my hand, to get my attention.

"Oh, yes I did, really weird by most standards." I said, after coming out of the thoughts I had been lost in.

"It's real busy this evening, so can you remember to catch me up next time I see you?" he asked.

"Sure, but I need to check out a few more things first." I explained. "I have tomorrow off and I am going to try to get Nell to help me." I added.

"Rita! I saved you a seat." I heard Nell's voice from the back of the bus.

Waving at Nell, I made my way to the back of the bus and sat down. "There seems to be a lot more people on the bus this evening," I said, "Thank goodness you always save me a seat, Nell," I giggled.

"I'm not sure where all of these people came from, but I agree, there does seem to be a lot of people this evening." she said.

Tapping the person on the shoulder in front of me, I asked, "Are all of you together and going somewhere special?"

Turning with a smile on his face, "Yes, there's going to be a special opening tonight at the Far Bar and a local band we all know is playing." he informed us.

"What kind of music?" Nell asked.

"I was told they were playing mostly Rock n' Roll with a little Jazz mixed in here and there, but they are good. Want to come?" he asked.

"What's the address?" I asked.

"It's 2213 Maple St., around the corner from the Baley's Market on Evergreen and it starts around 7pm." he offered.

Nell and I looked at each other and

smiled. "It might be fun, " I said.

"Yeah, I'm up for it," said Nell.

"Is there a cover charge?" I asked.

"Someone was saying they thought it was going to be about $3.dollars." he said.

"Thanks," Nell said as he turned back around and resumed talking to his friend.

"Ok, let's get down to it, catch me up on what has happened." she said looking at me with a grin.

"Do you remember my dream I had a while back? Well most of it that I remember, came true today. It was really wild to see it played out in real life." I explained.

"Wow, Really?" Nell questioned.

"Yeah, it was the strangest thing, I was putting away the dishes under the counter and there was Anna getting ready to sit down at one of the booths. I looked in the mirror at myself and then at her and found myself wishing I was there instead of where I was..." 'boy what a strange feeling.' I said explaining that part of my day.

"So do you want to go back to the Clair Mont tomorrow?" said Nell.

"Really? Me too." I said surprised. Then we both laughed. I believe we were both thinking the same thing. "What a mystery and it is close to being solved, at least I think so."

"Ok, so getting back to the music tonight. Do you want to meet me at my house since it is only about three blocks from me?" asked Nell.

"Ok, that sounds good. I will try to be there about 6:45 tonight." I said. "It won't take us anymore that a few minutes to walk there, right?"

"Sure, we can make it there in a few minutes." Nell agreed.

"Here's my stop, I'll see you in a little while." I said going toward the door. "Bye George," I yelled toward the front as I got off the bus.

"Hello Anna, how is my pretty girl." I asked while picking her up from the front step. That was one thing I could count on each evening after work. Anna was always waiting for me to take her up stairs.

Petting her while walking to our apartment I was telling her about my day. Anna was a great listener.

"Ok, we're home girl." I said as I put her on the couch on my way to change clothes. She jumped down and was right behind me, letting me know it was time to eat.

"I am going to fix us something to eat in a few minutes. You know I always change clothes when I first get home." I said while she was meowing. "You must be real hungry tonight." I added.

"Ok, let's go get something for you to eat while I fix dinner." I said heading for the kitchen.

I put water in a pan and then reached into the fridge for some milk for Anna and took out some hotdogs.

Placing the bowl of milk on the floor,

I said "Here you go, Anna, there is something to hold you till I can get dinner done."

"Boy you must have really been hungry. I guess you didn't catch anything today, huh?" I asked while she hurriedly drank and jumped up on the chair and asked for more. "You will just have to wait a few more minutes and I will give you half of a hot dog with your regular dinner" I said stroking her head and neck.

Taking the mustard and onion from the fridge got to be a chore with Anna's tail wrapped around my legs, but I managed to get them to the table. Grabbing a bowl and a knife I started preparing the onion for the hotdog when I noticed that Anna was now standing on the chair with her front paws on the table.

"Now you know better than to get on the table, Anna. How far are you planning to go?" I said looking straight at her.

She meowed and moved her head in

a way that made her look like she was trying to point at the onion. "What am I doing? I'm cutting an onion. Ok. I will give you a little, but I don't think you're going to like it much." I said, putting two very small piece of onion in front of her on the table.

She stiffed them, stuck out her tongue to touch one, and drew her tongue back in quickly, shaking her head she jumped down.

I had to laugh. She was still shaking her head while walking silly and making herself dizzy from all of the head shaking. "You silly girl, you are so funny. Here let's give you a small drink of milk to get the taste of onion off your tongue." I said pouring just a little milk in her bowl.

Chapter Eight

"Are you ready for half a hotdog, because they are ready for us?" I asked while taking them out of the pot and empting the water into the sink.

I placed mine on my plate with the bun and all the fixings, then placed hers in her food bowl and opened a can of her food and gave her a little of it too. "There you go. This is all you get, so don't eat it fast. I'm going to go out tonight, so I won't be here to give you anything extra." I informed her.

"Wow time went fast Anna. I guess we were having fun. I have to go get dressed so I can meet Nell and go listen to music." I said, looking at the clock again as I took my last bite.

Anna took her last bite and followed me to the bedroom. "Anna, I am going to put the TV on to keep you company while I am gone." I informed her while she jumped up on the bed.

I turned on the TV and reached under the bed for her ball. "Ok, you have the TV on and your ball to play with. I should be back in a few hours. So you be good and stay out of trouble." I said.

I grabbed my jacket and locked the door on my way out.

Walking to Nell's I got a chance to think about all that had happened at work earlier. *'Wow, I can hardly wait till tomorrow.'* I thought.

Nell answered her door just as I started to knock. "Right on time!" she said.

"Ready to go?" I asked.

"Yep!" she said grabbing her coat. "This is a nice night to be taking a walk." she added.

"I agree, it's not too warm or cold. The wind isn't blowing much and it's not raining. It's just one of those nice spring nights." I said laughing. "So what do you think about what happened at work today?" I asked.

"The more I think about it the more I know you are weird like Me." she said laughing.

"Well I like that!" I said putting my hands on my hips and sort of stepping away from her. "Look who's talking." I laughed.

We joked and laughed all the way there. At the bar the music was loud, but good energizing and the people were all friendly.

"Well that was a nice few hours." said Nell on our way back to her house.

"So are we going to go back to the Clair Mont, tomorrow? I asked.

"I sort of figured we would show up over there around noon and maybe eat lunch there. Something on the low priced end of the menu." she laughed.

"Ok, sounds good to me. So, I need to be here by 10:00 AM Right?" I asked.

"That sounds about right. That way we will have enough time for the busses to run, with a few minutes to spare." she informed me.

Sleep came hard for some reason. I laid there and stared at the dots on my bedroom ceiling for hours before I finally fell asleep.

Morning came too soon but my Anna was full of energy. She bounced onto the bed and headed straight for my pillow. She walking over to me and put her little wet nose on mine to let me know it was time to get up. "Ok, baby girl, I'm getting out of bed." I said moving to what seemed to be the speed of syrup on a cold morning.

Anna was meowing as she started for the bedroom door, urging me to hurry up so she could eat. "Ok, Ok, I'm working on it. I'll be there, just give me a minute." I said laughing while heading into the bathroom.

Opening the door to the bathroom, I almost stepped on Anna's tail. She had sat herself down right in front of the bathroom door and was waiting on me to come out. "What? You think I have to be guided to the kitchen? You silly, lovable girl you." I said picking her up and giving her a hug. "You're really loved, but you know that, don't you?" I said. "I think even you would have a hard time believing the dreams I've been having the last few weeks." I added.

Purring and meowing at the same time, she sounded like she was trying to talk. "You are such a funny little girl." I said giving her another hug while walking into the kitchen.

I put her on the floor and started getting breakfast for both of us. I put our breakfast on the TV trays and headed for the living room to watch a little news before heading to Nell's.

"Anna!" I said surprised. "That is one of the people I had a dream about a few nights ago." As I listened to the story, I found out that he was an art dealer in

France and had just bought a painting from a new artist. Then they told what he paid for it, "WOW! A half a million dollars for one painting? What a trip." I said as my fork dropped onto my plate with a clatter.

"Boy Anna, that makes me want to learn how to paint." I said with a giggle. "Well girl, it is getting close to that time. I'm going to spend time with Nell today." I said turning off the TV in the middle of the story and heading for the bedroom.

Within a few minutes, Anna had found her mouse and was playing with it on the bed.

"Ok Anna, get ready to go outside and play for a few hours? Come on baby." I said as I picked her up.

As I went out the door, I grabbed my light jacket and locked the door behind me. I took Anna down stairs and placed her on one of the wide banisters instead of the step.

"Now you be good today and I will be back as soon as I get things done." I said.

Walking over to Nell's gave me a chance to think about all the weird dreams I was starting to remember. And that little bit of news that I heard was enough to bring back some of the dreams.

Getting closer to Nell's house, I could see that her windows were open. "HEY NELL! I'm here." I said loud enough for her to hear. She came to the door with an energetic bounce in her step.

"You will never guess what I have remembered." I said.

"Well I feel good about today. So come on in and tell me what you remember." she said opening the door for me. "Want some tea or a soda?" she continued as we walked into the kitchen.

"Some tea sounds good." I said sitting down at the table and watched while she filled the tea kettle with water.

"So tell me what you remember." She said turning to look at me, then put the kettle on the burner.

"Well, I was watching TV this morning and they were showing a man in France that bought this painting that he paid a half mill for.

Then they showed a blip of the painting in the background and that is when I remembered seeing him in a dream a few nights ago and it was as if I was the one that painted the painting.

And I remember a few others too and another painting. I turned off the TV in the middle of the story because it was just hitting a little too close to the feeling I was getting from the painting at The Rooster. You know what I mean?" I asked.

"Well I watched the rest of that news story, the one you are talking about and that man is very wealthy and he is coming to see the rest of this artist's paintings. And guess where the artist lives?" she asked with a short pause. "Yes, right here in New York. What do you think about that?" she said, placing two cups on the table.

"You mean he **is** coming to New York to see more of the painting by this artist?" I asked, just to make sure that I heard it right.

"Yep, that's what the news said." replied Nell.

"I bet I know who he's coming to see too. I think he's coming to see Anna." I said.

"You know I think you may be right." she agreed. "After we finish our tea, how about you and me go see if Anna is home?" she continued.

"That sound real good, I would love to go see the rest of what she has done, art wise and I would love to find out just who or when she is." I agreed.

"So what do you mean "when she is?" Nell asked.

"Well so far, each one of the dreams I have had about all this, have come true. And if the one I had the other night, after watching

"Time Machine" on the SiFi channel,

comes true, then Anna came from some other time." I said finishing my tea with a giggle.

"All right-ee then, well I guess we will see then," Nell said laughing. Taking her last swallow, she said. "Well, I'm ready to go see if your dreams pan out. Are you ready for the showdown?" she asked with a big smile.

"OK! Then Let's do it. I'm ready." I said getting up and putting my cup in the sink.

"Well then we are off, and just on time if I may say so myself, George will be by in about eight minutes." she said as we walked to the front door.

We grabbed our jackets and Nell made sure the door was locked. We got to the bus stop in time to wait for about two minutes for the bus.

"Hi George." we both said at almost the same time, laughing as the bus doors opened.

"Hi gals, so where are you two headed today?" he asked.

"We are headed for the Clair Mont." declared Nell as I put the money in the box.

"Don't forget your transfers then." he said handing me the transfers as we headed down the aisle.

"We will let you know all about our findings when we get to the bottom of all this. I promise." I said looking back at him and almost stepping on Nell's heels. She had stopped in front of me to keep from falling over someone's backpack.

"Looks like the bus is full again." she said, looking over her shoulder at me.

"Well, hang on girls." George said looking through his mirror at us, as we laughed and reached for the slings hanging over head.

As the bus got closer to our stop, it filled up with people, making it hard to see when we were getting close to our stop. Soon, we heard George shouting over all the noise of the bus.

"Hey Girls! Here is your stop." he said while bringing the bus to a stop.

"Thanks George, we couldn't see where we were." I said.

"Sort of figured that when I got to where I couldn't see you in the crowd. Your next bus will be here is a few minutes, Tell Lynn I said hi, OK?" he said as he opened the back door of the bus. "My last run is at 6pm, make sure you catch me. I want to know what you find out." he said laughingly as we got off.

"Ok, we can do that." said Nell, waving as he closed the door.

We walked toward the bus stop and had just sat down and relaxed when Lynn's bus came to a stop in front of us.

"Hi Lynn, George said to tell you hi from him." " So hi!" I said repeating myself.

"Here are the transfers," said Nell while taking them from my hand with a giggle. Looking around we found a place to sit right up close to Lynn.

Chapter Nine

"So, George tells me that you two are checking out a mystery. How is it going?" Lynn asked.

"Pretty good that's why we are going back to the Clair Mont again today." volunteered Nell.

The rest of the ride was relaxing, no conversation and there were only a few people on the bus, all sitting quietly reading or napping.

"Here you are, this is your stop and my last run today is at 4:50 pm." said Lynn.

"Thanks and we will let you know too, if we find out anything." I said as we stepped off the bus.

Heading down the street, Nell looked over at me and started laughing,

"What!" I said starting to laugh too.

"Didn't we do this a few weeks ago? Or was that some people that just looked like us?" asked Nell and we both started busting up with laughter.

"Uh, maybe we are just dreaming and this is all really in our minds." I said and started humming the tune from one of our favorite SiFi shows.

Arriving at the Clair Mont, Nell looked at me and said "Boy that was quick."

"I think it just seemed quick because we knew where we were going," I said with a chuckle.

"Look! There's Danny," Nell said a little louder than normal, pointing toward the elevators.

"Danny!" We both said loud enough for him to hear but at the same time trying not to disturb anyone else. "Wait up" I said.

"Hi Rita! Hi Nell! What are you two doing here?" Danny asked.

"We came to see Anna. Can you take us to her room?" I asked.

"Well first, we have to go to the desk and have them ring her room and ask permission to go up." he said leading the way to the lobby desk.

"These ladies would like to speak to Ms. Anna Stolks." he told the desk clerk, who's back was turned to us at the time.

"Yes of course," he said as he turned around. But as he seen me he started to smile. "You caught me, I though there really was someone to see Ms. Anna Stolks." he said laughing. "Good day Ms. Anna." he said looking at me.

"No, I'm not Anna, I'm Rita." I said matter-of-factly.

The desk clerk looked over at Danny, as if to say "What is going on here.?"

"This is Miss Anna's sister, Rita." explained Danny.

"Of course you are. How silly of me, I should have known, because you look a lot like her. You must be twins." he said, trying to keep the blush out of his face. "I am so sorry, I will ring her room immediately." he said turning toward the switchboard.

"Hello Ms. Anna? Rita and her friend...uh...." he said pausing long enough to look back at us for Nell's name.

"Nell" I said.

Turning back to the phone, he said "Nell are here to see you. Yes ma'am, right away."

Hanging up the phone, he turned around and looked at Danny. "You may take them up to Ms. Anna's room, she is expecting them." he said waving his hand at Danny in a hurry up motion.

"Yes Sir, Right away." said Danny motioning for us to follow him. "I'll take you to Miss Anna's room." he said looking back over his shoulder at us.

Walking toward the elevator, Nell and I looked at each other and giggled.

Danny looked back at us, and as he pushed the button he looked himself over to make sure we weren't laughing at him.

"You're fine Danny, we are just thinking of what Anna's response to us will be. It has been a long while since she has seen me." I explained.

"I think she will like to see you, after all she did ask for you to come to her room." he said.

Just then the elevator doors opened, "Well this is the floor, and right up here is her door," he said pointing as we stepped out of the elevator and followed him up the hall.

"This is it," he said knocking on the door.

Anna opened the door with a big smile, "Hello Danny, Thank you for bringing them up to see me. Here is a little something for you." she said putting out her hand toward Danny.

"No, No, Miss Anna, that's not necessary, it was my pleasure." he said.

"You will take this or I will have to get mean with you," she said with a smile.

Nell and I looked at each other, not sure what she meant by that remark. I thought I might know, but wasn't really sure.

He reached out his hand with a small chuckle and took what she had in it and said thanks with a slight bow.

"Come on in," Anna said looking over at us. "He's a great kid, last time he said no, I made him come in and eat four cookies, after each one I asked him if he was ready to take the present I was trying to give him, and after the fourth he finally said yes. We got a good laugh out of it and I told him not to make me get mean with him again," she explained.

"Good deal," said Nell with a sigh of relief.

"So what brings you here to see me, as if I didn't know." she said with a laugh.

"I work at the Rooster Cafe where" I started to explain.

"Yes I know, that's where one of my

paintings is hanging," she interrupted. "I was there just the other day, you saw me. I met up with Charlie and you know he hasn't changed a bit from what I remember of him." she continued.

Nell and I were looking a little puzzled, I guess.

"Come sit down, for this I will need to start at the beginning." she said as she lead us into her sitting room.

Mandy came out of the other room, "Would you like for me to ring the kitchen for you Ms. Anna?" she asked.

"Would either of you like to have a drink or a snack?" Anna asked, looking at us.

"Not right now, thank you though." I said

"Check back with me in about an hour, Mandy," she said as Mandy gave a slight curtsy and left the room.

"Now to tell you the whole story." she said as she sat down in a chair across from us.

"I think this may be a little hard for you to follow at first, so if you get lost at any time, stop me and ask any questions you may have," she explained. "This whole thing started about three years ago when I turned 69 years old. In the time line I came from." she said.

"Woe, wait a minute, _Your_ time line?" Nell questioned.

"Yes, well you see, I wasn't, well sort of was, born in this time line. It is a little confusing to those who haven't experienced it." Anna tried explaining.

"You know, come to think about it, maybe I had better start at the very beginning and you may be able to understand it better. Rita and I are not really twins. When I knew I was coming back here I had the paper work all changed ahead of time by some of our peoples that are already in place. You see we have people in place all over the world in all time periods to help with the little details that we have to get into place before anyone is allowed to transport through time. I was born over 72 years ago as you, Rita May Stolks. As I went through my years and saw the way things happened, I didn't like the way it had been going. There were a lot of things I wished I could have done in my life but never seemed to have the time or money to do them.

One of these things was to be able to paint, so when I got to my 50th year I decided to take some real painting lessons, then I branched out on my own and everyone liked my artwork. That is to say I had tried to learn from some books and took a few classes in the local college but nothing like I took when I was 50. After that I decided to come back to this time period to live for a while, to add a little more points to my account. That way I can do a few more things I always wanted to do."

"Points?" I interrupted.

"Yes, points are the way we count our wealth in my time period. Everyone was in the point system by 2023. Anyway one of the things I wanted to do was to have enough funds to do things I always wanted to do and didn't have time to because I was always working.

Just by talking to you like this now may change things in my lifetime where I came from. So I am asking you to do a few things for me and I need for you to promise this to me. OK?" she asked.

"Okay, what do you need me to do?" I asked.

Chapter Ten

"When I was in school and asked to draw or paint something, my mind always seemed to go blank and I would end up just staring at the paper. But I imagine you have already started feeling like you wish you could paint now that you can see what can be done. I guess you could take a few basic lessons, but not to many. Because the way you will learn in the future will be a little more productive. If you learn the ways they paint now, you won't be open to new ways, and it will make it harder for you to learn this way of painting. Also in about 1 year from today, you will need to invest this amount of money in this stock, no more and no less, and no later or earlier. Do you understand? I will seal it in this envelope and mark the date outside so it looks like a code." she said handing me a sealed envelope dated 17 year from today with "DO NOT OPEN TILL 3282021!" "And don't look at it till that date." Okay?" she added.

"Okay!" I said taking the envelope from her hand and trying not to touch her, because in all of the time travel movies I had watched touching the person from the future lead to bad trouble for both of them.

She noticed that. "Rita, don't worry, in the future they have a way to change the body that is going back so that if you meet yourself and give yourself a hug, nothing happens. In a big way we are the same as twins. I bet you have been having flashes of things I have done and people I have met for about the last month or so and didn't know what to think." she said.
"Yes, I thought I was going out of my mind, till Nell went and got a copy of my birth record and it said I was a twin. That mixed me up for a good while, because I remember

reading my birth record before and it said single birth. I read it again and again thinking that I was missing something but it always read the same. Saying that I was a single birth until about, what three months ago, Nell?" I questioned, looking over at Nell.

"Yes, about that." she said, with a look of total wonder on her face.

"Ok, now since we took care of that part of it. I can tell you the rest of the story." Anna continued. "We were pretty much twins from about a year ago. That is when I started going through the classes and the changes so I could come back and do things without hurting either of us. In any of the dreams you have had, did you remember meeting this guy?" she questioned, "Or these two people?" she said showing me three drawings of people.

"Yes. That one looks like someone I had a dream about, but he had a scar on his face, just under his chin." I informed her. "I also had one about the guy that bought your last painting when you were in France." I added.

"Oh yeah that. Well that was a lot of fun, and he is coming here to see some others that I have painted. This is something that just happened. Getting a painting sold to Charlie was something I planned to do, because I remembered he had always wanted something, to bring in customers when I worked there and he never found anything, so I never got my raise. My plan was to change things a little so I wouldn't have to get a loan for this trip in my future, if that makes any since." she said with a chuckle.

"The other guy that you had a dream about was my art teacher. He is the one that taught me the way I paint now. It was funny because he taught me how to pain by telling me what to do. But he could never get it to work for himself. Before I was just painting the way everyone else did and my paintings didn't make a big difference in any one's lives. But since this guy taught me this new way of painting I am able to really do things like I have always wanted too. Oh, this guy's name is Master Bastrono and he will save you a lot of time and energy. You will be able to find him in about 4 years in San Francisco, California. He will own a little art shop near the hospital." she added.

"WOW, in just 4 years?" I questioned.

"Yes, I didn't come back very far, just a few years, a little over 41 years from my time." She chuckled. "The short jots are easier to handle, and when our medical team make the changes in our body, it doesn't hurt and you get to be younger than you were." she said laughing.

"Younger?" I asked.

"Well yes, right here right now I am the same age as you, but for real I am 72 years of age in my time, but shuuusssh! Don't tell anyone." she said giving such a laugh that Nell and I couldn't help but laugh too.

"Do you want to see my other paintings? I will be showing them to the guy from France tomorrow?" she asked while laughing.

"Yes please!" Nell and I said almost in unison.

"I have them stored in my closet. Come on and I will let you see them." she said as she got up then motioning for us to follow here into the bedroom.

Just as we got up to follow her, someone knocked on the door.

"Just a moment, let me find out who this is. On second thought, I bet it's Mandy." she said looking at her watch. "Do you girls want anything to eat or drink, it is getting close to lunchtime." she added.

"Well, maybe a light lunch and maybe a soda." I said looking at Nell for a nod.

"Ok then that is what it will be," she said as she opened the door.

"Hi Mandy, yes we are ready to order lunch, we would like to have three number two's and three drinks of your choice. Okay?" she said with Mandy writing it all down.

"Yes ma'am, and thank you," she said as she left.

Anna turned to walk toward the bedroom again. "Do you want to see <u>all</u> of the other paintings I have done so far? I also have photos of the ones I have sold." she offered.

"You don't have to ask us twice." said Nell.

"I have them in my bedroom, so come on," she said walking toward the next room. "Ok, sorry, stay right there and close your eyes." she said, looking at both of us.

Standing there in the doorway we closed our eyes and waited. We could hear some things being moved but couldn't tell by the sound what she was doing. "I think she's setting up the painting for us to look at." I whispered to Nell.

"Ok! You can open your eyes and come into the room the rest of the way." she said motioning for us to come and stand next to her.

There they were, the paintings were leaning against the wall, bed and dresser, even on top of the dresser, the two chairs and against the two nights stands. There were paintings of all sizes and shapes. I think, I would be safe in saying there were at least twelve paintings.

The one that stood out the most to me was one of a large autumn colored butterfly. But when I stepped up closer to it, I could see that it was really autumn colored trees and bushes with green ones in the background and a stream going across the corner of painting. The body of the butterfly was really the dead trunk of a very large old tree and its antenna were the two branches left at the top of the trunk.

"I like that one." I said pointing at the

one that looked like a butterfly.

"I do too, that is my favorite out of all of them," said Anna walking over to pick it up. "You know, I think this is the one that Monsieur DeJarnees will want to buy tomorrow. But it will be expensive because it is my favorite." she added.

"Monsieur DeJarnees?" asked Nell

"Yes, that's right," said Anna, "He bought my "Two Hand Shaking" for half a million dollars. I think I can get him to go a little higher on this one, if he likes it... I think my goal will be three-quarters of a million this time." she added.

Nell spoke up after hearing the knocking on the door over Anna and our laughter at the jokes we were sharing, "Anna! Someone is at your door."

"Oh, thanks. It must be Mandy with our lunches," she said smiling and heading for the door.

After eating and sharing a few more stories, Nell spoke out again. "Rita, if we don't leave very soon we will miss our buses."

"I will pay for you a taxi ride." offered Anna.

"No, that isn't necessary," I said, "Nell and I have a friend that drives one of the buses and he will want to know what happened today and we did promise to tell him about the mystery person that painted the painting hanging at The Rooster." I explained.

"Just don't tell him everything, OK?" said Anna in a pleading voice.

"Oh no, by all means, just that the artist of The Rooster's painting turned out to be my long lost sister. And now she is pretty much famous. That's all, OK?" I said wanting her to agree.

"Sisters? Yes, that sounds good," Anna said agreeing

"We really need to get going, we can come back on another day to visit, but right now- we really must leave." coached Nell.

"Yes, we really do," I said looking over at the clock on Anna's wall. "But I really want to know how it turns out with Mr. DeJarnees." I added.

"Well here take my phone number and give me a call...say tomorrow night?" she said while writing it down on a scratch pad and handing me the paper.

Nell reached over and grabbed my hand. "We have to go now!" she said with urgency in her voice.

"Bye, I'll call tomorrow," I said while almost being dragged down the hall and laughing.

"Later" shouted Anna.

Just then to elevator doors opened and we got on and soon found ourselves on the main floor. The way we left the Clair Mont, reminded me of the story of Cinderella and her glass slipper, when she left the palace at midnight.

In a short time we were at the bus stop meeting Lynn.

"Hi Lynn, boy I wasn't sure we were going to get back here in time to meet you. Are you running on time?" Nell said, putting our fares in the box.

"Yes I am." answered Lynn with a smile.

"Thanks Nell," I said.

"For what?" she asked.

"Well for being there for me and eye on the time like you did. Wow! What a day. I have a sister in a real odd and weird way." I said

"Boy, you can say that again. A sister that has a lot of money and can pretty much do whatever she wants and not have to worry about it. It makes me wish I lived in her time frame." whispered Nell.

"You are, you are just in the now, we'll get there sooner that you think." I said and we both laughed.

"You know you are right, what am I worried about?" she said with a long sigh and a big smile.

The bus ride seemed real short, and we found ourselves waiting on George.

"Are you going back over to see Anna tomorrow?" asked Nell.

"I was thinking about it. Can you go?" I asked.

"No I have to work the next three days. Let me know what happens." she said.

"Oh not to worry, you will know just as soon as I know anything. You know that, you're my best friend." I said reaching over and squeezing Nell's hand with a smile.

"Good, I was starting to feel like a third wheel." she said with a smile.

"Never! Sisters are cool and all that, but I have been an only child for far too long. With a very good friend, who has always been better than a sister, if I may add that." I said looking right straight at her and smiling.

Nell gave me a big hug just as George stopped the bus in front of us.

"Well I take it that you have some

news for Me." he said motioning for us to get on the bus.

"Yeah," I said, "Sure do"

"Ok, so give it up, I want to know all of it, everything." he said.

With a laugh I told him all that I thought would be ok, but nothing about where or when Anna came from.

"So does that mean you have money now?" he asked with a silly grin on his face.

"No! The money she got from her paintings is hers George, Gees, what makes you ask that?" I inquired.

Chapter Eleven

"Just had to tease you a little." he said laughing. "Fooled you huh?" he added. "I have a few friends that have got me started in the neighborhood theater, I am learning to act." he bragged.

We sat down right behind George.

"Well you had me fooled, I thought you were serious there for a minute" I said with a chuckle.

"Yeah, you had me fooled too." added Nell.

Looking out the window, Nell turned to me, "Did you know that we are already nearing our stops?"

"You have to be kidding me, already?" I questioned looking out the window myself in disbelief. "Wow that was quick."

"Time goes by fast when you are having fun. That is what I have always heard." said George.

"Well I guess we have been having fun then," I said as we all laughed.

"Ok, I will see you both tomorrow." I said with a wave as I got off the bus.

Soon I was at my front steps and Anna, my longtime friend was waiting there on the banister like normal.

"Hey kiddo, how did your day go?" I asked while picking her up on my way to our apartment. "Well, you will never guess what I did today." I said while I unlocked our door.

"There you go," I said putting her down on the couch. "I will fix us something to eat in a little while." I said heading for the bedroom to change.

"Meow! Meow!" Anna said as she jumped onto the bed.

"Ok, I am hurrying but, I have had a very busy day today." I informed her. "I know you are hungry. The way you are talking, one would think you hadn't eaten all day. You mean to tell me that Mr. Berealy didn't leave any meat scraps out today. I know he got lamb in today.

Well then, you will be eating good tomorrow from his shop." I said with a laugh.

Following me into the kitchen, she had her tail stroking my legs the whole way. "Now you know that when you stay under foot like that, you take a chance on getting stepped on. Go sit next to your bowl and I will give you some milk." I said pointing at her bowl.

When I turned around from getting the milk out of the frig, she was sitting very posed by her dish waiting.

"You sure are a smart cat," I said stroking her head and back, as I poured her milk into the bowl.

"There you go, drink it slow. It will take me a few minutes to get dinner done tonight." I said.

It didn't take her long to finish the milk and she was under foot again.

"Anna!" I said loudly to get her attention while picking her up. "You need to stay in here and watch TV for me, while I finish fixing dinner," I said while carrying her into the living-room and placing her on the couch. Turning on the TV, I flipped it to the news, "We are having sloppy-Joes and potatoes, so stay put, OK?" I added sort of in a scolding tone.

She jumped down, got her mouse and jumped back up onto the couch and was playing with it when I headed back into the kitchen where I had left dinner cooking.

Listening to the TV, I hurriedly put the rest of Anna's food on her plate when a story caught my attention.

"In the news today from France, Monsieur DeJarnees was showing off the newest art he bought from an unknown who lives in the United States. And yes, we will be showing it to you, but first a little more about Monsieur DeJarnees. He is a wealthy and very well-known art collector in the art circles of the world. He is known for being the man who helps to make the unknown artist, known, if not renowned. Now for a quick look at his newest art piece. It is called "Two Hands Shaking" said the announcer.

I ran to the living room just in time to see the painting. It was a painting of a pair of hands shaking hands with a lake in the back ground, from a distance.

"We just found out that the artist of this phenomenal painting is Anna May Stolks" he said proudly. "And when you get closer to the painting it changes, take a look." he said pausing so the cameraman could get a closer picture of the painting.

"You see what I mean, from a distance it is just two hands shaking hands, but now you can see, it turned out to be an old map." added the announcer.

"Anna! That's the second painting Anna, I mean I sold as my future self, the one at The Rooster Cafe was really the first painting I, I mean she, sold. This sounds really mixed up, doesn't it girl?" I said giving her a few strokes.

"You are such a great cat" I said, giving her a pat on the head, "that when I come back in the future I name myself after you. Now move over a little and I'll bring dinner in" I added while setting up her tray

She meowed politely and moved over.

"Ok, here is your dinner." I said, setting her plate on her tray and mine on my TV tray and I then sat down beside her, pulling my tray closer so I could eat comfortably.

"You know Anna, I think this dinner turned out pretty good. And no, I didn't put any sauce on yours. I remembered you didn't like it. "Right girl?" I questioned, giving her a stroke down her back.

We finished dinner, did the dishes, watched a little more TV and went to bed.

I was awakened in the early morning with the wind rattling the windows. Between the patter of rain tatting a rhythm to the wind it was almost like listening to music. I found myself drifting off to sleep again and that was okay because I didn't have to go to work.

The next thing I knew the phone was ringing and it was Nell.

"Oh hello Nell," I said after looking at the caller ID.

"Have you talked to Anna yet?" she asked in excitement.

"No, I thought I would wait till this evening. Why?" I asked.

"Well, I just heard that Mr. DeJarnees was going to meet with Anna at 10:00am this morning. And it is 1:30pm now." she explained.

"For Real? It's that late already?" I questioned.

"Yes! Did you sleep in today?" she asked with a giggle.

"Yes, I guess we did." I said trying not to yawn while answering. "Ok, I guess I will get dressed, eat and then call. Do you want me to call you later at work?" I asked.

"No, no, that's ok. I will talk to you later this evening." she said.

"Sure, OK!" I answered and we hung up.

"Wow, Anna, we were being sleepy heads this morning. Huh girl?" I said climbing out of bed.

Anna was already on her way to the kitchen.

"You know you have to wait on me, you silly girl." I said loudly so she could hear me from the kitchen.

"Meow! Meow!" came her answer.

"Ok, just thought I would remind you." I said while I finished dressing.

I flipped on the news on my way through the living room.

"Anna! Guess what, Mr. DeJarnees did buy the Butterfly painting." I said excited.

Not really sure why I would be excited, because all this was happening to my future self. None of this would be helping me right now, but somehow it was exciting.

I hurried breakfast and then I called the phone number on the paper Anna had given to me last evening.

"Anna! Congratulations! I just heard the news on the TV, about you selling Mr. DeJarnees the Butterfly painting." I said.

"You mean it has already hit the news? Why, we just finished the deal less than an hour ago. You know I'll bet the press and news people were down stairs waiting to see what he was going to buy." she said with excitement. "I am standing here holding a cashier's check for three million dollars." she added.

"Three Million? I thought you were

going to ask three/quarters of a million." I
questioned.

"I know but when he saw the rest of
the paintings, he bought 3 others and I am
having them transported to France today, by
airfreight." she explained.

"Wow! That is so great!" I said
excited for her.

"We need to talk about a few things. I
will send my car for you at 6:00pm. We can
have dinner and talk over a few things I
think you should know about." she said,
sounding serious.

"OK, that will give me time to catch
Nell up on what happened with the
paintings today. She called a little while ago
and was asking if I had talked to you yet." I
explained.

"Let me give you my address." I
offered.

"I have your address. I used to live
there, remember?" she said with a giggle.

"Oh yeah," I said joining in the

laughter.

"Till then... Bye" I said as I hung up the phone.

Time went by fast. I made a quick call to Nell and told her all that had happened and that I was having dinner with Anna tonight. We agreed to get together tomorrow after work.

I had just finished making my Anna's dinner and placed it on her tray just as heard a knock at the door.

"Now Anna, here is your dinner and the TV is on for you. You be a good girl for me tonight. I'm not sure what time I will be home, but it may be late." I explained while petting her.

"I'll be right there." I shouted as the second knock came.

I grabbed my jacket, stuck my wallet and keys in my pocket and headed for the door.

"Hello." I said opening the door.

"Hello, I am Anna's driver. You must

be Rita, Anna's twin sister?" he said.

Chapter Twelve

He was a rather nice looking fellow. Very tall with sandy brown hair and deep green eyes. He looked like he worked out and liked the sun.

"Oh sorry. My name is James. I will be your driver for this evening." he said with a shallow bow and a large smile.

"Thank you James, I am glad to meet you." I said, smiling back.

We went down stairs and out to the car, were he opened the limousine's door for me. I climbed in and chose to sit up close to the window that divided the front of the limo from the back.

He closed the door and promptly walked around the limo and got in. He rolled down the window that was between us.

"So James, how long have you

known Anna?" I asked.

"Oh, I think it is going on about twelve years now." he said, glancing back at me through the mirror.

Well, I guess he could see that, this bit of information was a shock to me and he let out a soft laugh.

"Has she told you very much about what has happened in the last four years?" he questioned, looking back at me.

"Well a little, but I'm sure she hasn't told me everything yet. So did you come with her to New York?" I asked.

"Yes, but I think I should wait and let her tell you the rest of the story." he said with a wink and a smile.

It didn't take long and we were driving up to the front of the Hotel.

James got out, walked around to my side of the limo, opened the door and then offered his hand to help me out.

I took his hand and surprisingly enough it really did make it easier to get out of the limo.

"You know how to get to Anna's Suite, right?" he asked politely with a smile.

"Yes, I remember that part. Thank you James." I said turning to go into the hotel.

I glanced back at him over my shoulder and he was watching me till I went through the hotel door. Then got back into the limo and drove away.

The desk clerk phoned Anna and told her I was on my way up.

She was standing just outside her door when I got off the elevator.

"Hi Rita, how was your ride over?" she asked.

"Great, but I am confused a little. James says he has known you for about twelve years. How can that be?" I asked as we went into her suite.

"Well that is a good story and part of what I want to talk to you about tonight. Come on in, I have ordered dinner for us and it will be her in about half an hour." she said with a smile.

I sat down on the couch and Anna sat in her favorite chair as Mandy brought in two sparkling waters and two glasses with ice on a silver tray.

"Thank you Mandy." Anna said. "I think that is all we will need till our dinner arrives." she explained.

"Thank you Miss Anna. Then I'll join the others downstairs in the kitchen." she said with a shallow curtsy, then headed for the front door.

"Now, I have a few things I feel I need to let you in on, and yes it may change a few things, but hopefully for the good." Anna stated while looking over at me.

"So, is there really a chance of changing things in the future if I learn things from you now?" I asked, concerned.

"You know that there is a chance of the future changing even if you were to look in the wrong direction at the wrong time.

The future is always changing. Our lives are what we make of them. Things are constantly changing, we can't stop that. When I go back to the time line I came from, my life will have changed from how I left it. This time I will have the money to pay for this trip myself and I wouldn't have to borrow it. You did put that letter I gave you in a safe place, right?" she asked, sounding concerned.

"Yes, I did just like you told me." I said. "I also added a very small dot in an area only I will notice." I added, "Just in case."

"Good then that part is in place. Now you make sure you follow the instructions to the letter. OK?" she instructed.

"Okay." I answered.

"Now, as far as me knowing James. That story is the main reason I wanted you to come tonight. You see, in the future, when you are about 59 years of age there will be an earthquake in the area where you will be living, which is ok because you will be happy living there. You have a lot of friends and an art business you have fun with. So not to worry about any of that, but during the quake, I got hurt. Or maybe I should say you may get hurt, because we don't know how much of the future will be changed by what I have already put into place with the envelope I told you to hold onto."

"So anyway, my back got injured, and there was a time where I had to have a lot of help just to get around. That is when I met James and we became very good friends." Anna explained.

"Yes I could tell that by the way he said he had known you for around twelve years." I said with a laugh.

"At the time I got hurt, I was very lucky because the medical association was making headway in the transplanting of individual vertebrae and inter-vertebral cartilage. I was one of their first experiments. I have to say they did a very good job." she said, standing up and stooping over and touching her toes. "When I got hurt, they took x-rays of course, to find out how bad it was. I was told that two of the lumbar vertebrae in my lower back, were cracked and I had chipped one of the cervical, that's the ones in the neck area. Anyway, I had so much pain I couldn't move without screaming. I was told not to move or I could cut the spinal cord and then I wouldn't be able to walk or move at all for a very long time. Well they didn't have to tell me again, I remained very still. It took the Doctors and the Techs a week to get the vertebrae and cartilage ready for me. They had to make them from a synthetic material with what is called a 3-D printer. I have pictures of them if you want to see." she said pulling a book out of the bottom drawer of the end table near her.

"Yes, please. I would love to see what you are talking about. Because right now they just want to fuse the vertebrae together and make the back stiff." I said.

She sat down near me so we could both see the pictures at the same time. She opened the book, and there was a picture and a news clipping.

"Let me tell you when I first heard about this idea it was just before the quake. I found out even more later. The Doctors had been working on it for a while before the news got out. I liked the idea and followed their progress for a long while.

I was offered the chance to be the first person they put it in. I mean the new vertebrae that are in my back right now are made out of the same material that they will be working with in your time line soon for replacing joints, except for a few small changes. My new intervertebral discs are made from a very thick type of rubber cushion that the immune system will accept. The vertebrae start out in three to four pieces, this way they can be placed around

the spinal cord and the nerves. As you can
see in the drawing here there is a special clip
that hooks them together.

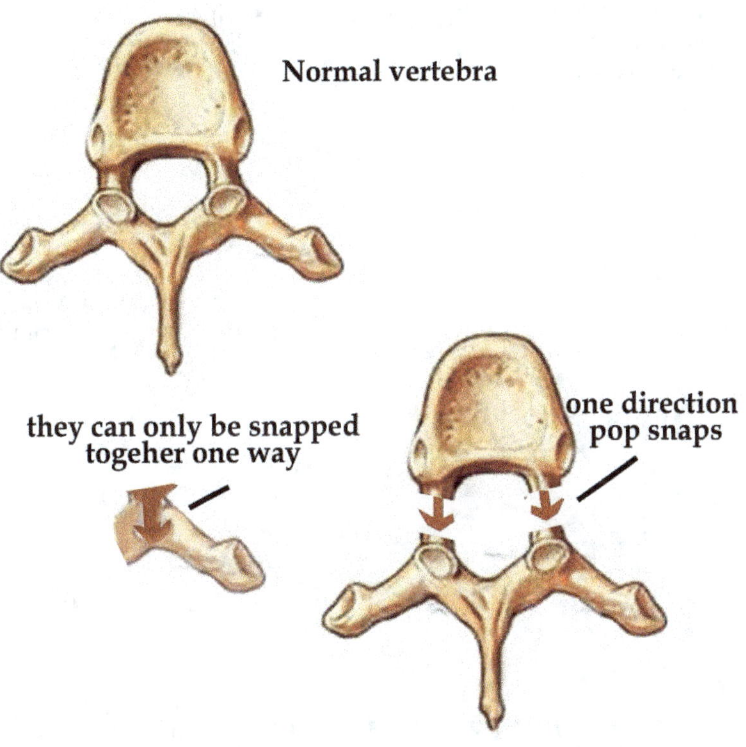

When the two pieces are placed
together, they can't be taken apart again,
without cutting them apart, at which point
they are no longer any good. The clip is sort
of like an internal pop snap. The
intervertebral disc also snaps into place and
helps cushion the natural vertebrae and the

man-made vertebrae.

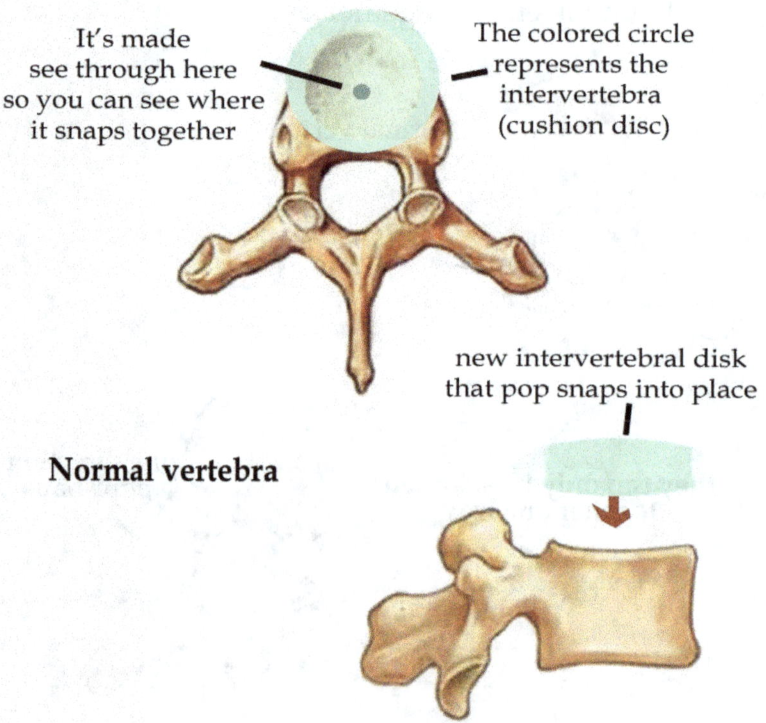

Each vertebrae and intervertebral are coated on all the areas where flesh would normally be connected to the real ones, with the imitation skin and pig skin is used to cover parts of them in some cases." she said looking at me. "Oh you know. The kind they use for burn victims, to help grow new skin.

I have full movement and there is no pain and they have a wearing time of 50 years." she explained.

"Wow. You know I think if there wasn't so much importance put on money, then the medical association could have come up with this faster." I said. "That reminds me of another question. In your time line, do the officials, you know, the bigwigs of the governing offices in DC, still get paid all the money they want and only push the laws that will help them or their friends and family?" I asked.

"No in fact, if you want to run for a public office, you have to prove you can survive on what the lower income people have and without another help." Anna paused and took a sip of water. " Your bank accounts and assets are all frozen till you pass the test and if you are caught getting help from friends or family, you are not allowed to run for any office for ten years, because that is considered cheating. At the beginning of this test, they are given $100 and the clothes on their back, noting else. At the end of eighteen months if they have, (on their own without any loans), a place to live and a good steady job and can meet all of their financial requirements each month, then they are allowed to run for office." She leaned back against a satin pillow. "Then when you get into office, you clock in and out each day and all entrances and exits are on camera, so if you leave without clocking out, you are docked four hours of your pay, this was put into place to keep the congress and senators and other officials from clocking in and then leaving to go play golf. When you leave and say it is for business, you are required to take one of the interns with you and it can't be the same one all the time. The intern is required to take a vocal and visual recording of everything that is said or done and if there is any time missing, then they are docked that amount of time twice." She learned over and picked up her water and took another sip. I did the same. "You know, when we put this into place, it seemed that the budges for the country and each of the states could take care of all they needed to do. Each official is given a good wage and they have to pay for all their own bills, just like everyone else in the country." she said getting up to answer the door.

I hadn't even heard the knock on the door. I was so taken by all that she had been telling me.

Chapter Thirteen

"Come to the table, dinner is here." she said motioning for me to come over where she was now standing.

Mandy was placing the food on the table and making sure that all of the dinnerware was in place.

"Miss. Anna, I took the liberty of getting you a juice cocktail and two other drinks to go with your meal." said Mandy with a smile.

"Mandy, you amaze me. You are so on top of things." Anna said. "Isn't she great?" she asked looking at me.

"I think you have a gem here, Anna." I said smiling at Mandy.

"I thank you both and I will return in about one hour for the plates and with dessert." said Mandy as she left with a curtsy.

"Thank you" said Anna as Mandy shut the door.

"Wow this meal looks great, like a king's feast." I said looking over the table.

The table was set with a beautiful spring-green salad, honey roasted carrots, green beans sprinkled with garlic and rosemary and pickled beets and butter roses. In the center of the table lying on a silver platter was a set of boneless chicken breast with small red potatoes surrounding it and herbal cream sauce on the side. A red platter near the chicken had fresh sliced French bread. There was also a choice of a mixed fruit juice, lite wine and sodas all on ice. Anna told me that the dessert was to be a surprise and I had to wait to find out what it was.

We talked about things we both remembered and that was fun and what the differences were in her time and in my time. I found that I enjoyed talking to my older self. It was a little like talking to a long lost friend. She asked about old friends and about Anna our cat. We talked of new inventions and old ones that had been improved, but I was told I couldn't tell anyone much of what we had talked about because it may change the future time line to much too fast and I agreed.

Mandy came back to gather the dishes and left us with an open faced watermelon stuffed with all manner of tropical fruit and butter cookies as a side dish. We talked for a few more hours before I noticed the time.

"That was the best meal I have ever had. But I don't think I will have to eat for a week. I am so full" I said laughing and patting my stomach.

Anna caught me looking at my watch. "It is getting late and I am starting to feel tired." I said.

"Not to worry Rita, when you get home our Anna will be asleep on your bed as usual. She is a great cat. I miss her. I will call James and let him know to bring the limo around to the front door in about ten minutes. Is that ok?" she asked.

"Yes, that sounds good," I agreed

"Oh, here, I almost forgot to give you this. I had Mandy make it up special." She added handing me a small covered dish. "It's for our baby girl."

"You remembered how much we worry about Anna? She is getting up in age and when she goes I will miss her very much." I said.

"Yes I know, I have already gone through that, I never got another cat, I was so spoiled by her." Anna replied.

"Here is your jacket and if you don't mind I will walk you out to the limo to meet James. I will be leaving your time in three days. It will take that long to get all the art sales settled." she said.

"There is so much more I would like to know. Please can't you stay a little longer?" I pleaded.

"No, Time is a harsh mistress and my promises must be kept. I arranged all of the time arrivals and departures ahead of time and they

must be kept. This is sort of like catching a train or airplane, except there is only one of them to catch." she said with a slight chuckle, as we walked out the front door to meet James.

We gave each other hugs and I climbed into the back of the limo and James drove me back to my apartment house.

"Here we are Miss. Rita," James announced.

"Thank you James," I said reaching for the door handle.

"No! No, mustn't touch the door handle. That is My Job!" James said trying to make a point.

"Oh! Ok, "I said with a giggle.

"Thank you, it has been a privilege to meet and drive you around this evening,

Miss. Rita." he said after opening the door for me and offering me his hand again then giving a bow.

"Well, thank you James. I have had a lot of fun tonight and have enjoyed every moment." I said looking into his eyes. "I can see why Anna likes having you as a friend and helper" I added as I finished climbing out of the limo.

James hurried past me to open the apartment house door for me.

"Thank you again and good night James. I will see you soon." I said with a wink as I went through the door and waved good bye to him.

He got into the limo and drove away. I hurried upstairs to see my baby girl, Anna. I had enjoyed my time with Anna, my other self, but at the same time I missed my little Anna.

I unlocked the door trying not to make any noise, just to see if Anna was asleep on my bed. Sure enough there she was sound asleep, curled up in a ball on the pillow next to mine.

Pulling off my jacket and tossed it on the couch and put Anna's gift in the refrigerator for tomorrow then headed for the bedroom. Sitting down on the bed I took off my shoes and got ready for bed. Anna woke up and "meow" her hello and asked for a snack by jumping off the bed and running toward the kitchen. I gave her some milk and told her I was going to bed and she could join me when she got through.

It wasn't long before she bounced onto the bed and took her place next to me on her pillow, and there she slept all night. I reached over and petted her. "Good night baby girl." I said.

She let out a soft meow and we both fell asleep.

Strange and intense would prove to be good words to describe the next few days.

A fresh spring breeze drifting

through my open window as the sun came streaming through. Anna and I both gave a big stretch before getting out of bed.

Anna managed to get to the kitchen before me. Looking up at me she was meowing for her breakfast. Wrapping her tail around my legs and slowing me down. "Anna, I know you are hungry, but you need to go by your dish and wait."

She meowed and did as I asked her.

Working fast I had to get our breakfasts fixed and get dressed. In my haste to get to sleep, I had forgotten to set my alarm. I had to catch George in about forty-five minutes.

Eating fast, I finished my breakfast, and hurried to the bathroom. Stepping out of the shower, I almost fell over Anna.

"Baby girl, I have to hurry, and you're getting under foot is not helping. Please go sit on the bed, I have to get dressed and catch George in about twenty minutes." I explained. Turning around she ran for the bed.

Finally I was dressed. I knew my keys and wallet were in my jacket, so I picked up Anna and grabbed my jacket as I headed for the door.

I placed Anna on the banister as I always have. "Now Anna you be a good girl today and stay safe. Ok? Love you." I said giving her a hug before hurrying to catch George.

As I hurried to catch the bus, I remembered that I had left my new bus pass on my dresser. *"Gee I hope he lets me on today."* I thought.

I got to the bus stop at the same time George did. "Hi George" I said as the bus doors opened.

"I saw you running, I almost got here first," said George with a laugh.

"George, I have a small problem this morning, uh," I stammered.

"What, Rita, what did or didn't you do this time?" ask George, trying to look serious.

"Well, I forgot the new bus pass in my other jacket." I said after taking a deep breath.

"Well get on the bus, I will just punch it twice tomorrow." said George, with a smile.

"You sure seem to be in a good mood this morning. What is going on," I asked.

"What do you mean? I'm always in a good mood, when I see you." he said with even a bigger smile.

"But you seem to be extra happy this morning." I said trying to get him to tell what happened.

"Ok, I'll tell you and then you can tell Nell, but no one else, OK?" he said, trying once again to look serious. "I got a fifteen cent raise, per hour." he said then busted into laughter. "It feels so good to know I can have a little left after the bills. Do you know what that means? That means that I can go somewhere on my next vacation." he said with this very large smile, backed with a chuckle.

"I am so glad for you! I can't think of anyone I would have liked to see get a raise more than you. You are the best bus driver I have ever known." I said with a smile.

"Thank you." he replied with an earnest expression.

As I turned to walk to the back of the bus, I spotted Nell. "Hi Nell, I went to see Anna last night. She sent James over with the Limo to pick me up and we had the most amazing dinner in her suite!" I said with a big smile.

"And?" Nell eagerly asked.

By the time I finished telling her about Anna's back injury and, the new procedure we were coming up on my stop.

"We'll talk this evening on the way home." I said getting off the bus.

"Later!" called Nell.

"Bye George." I said waving as he drove away.

I had about thirteen minutes before I had to clock in at work. I went in and took a glass of root beer to the back room with me. I figured I would drink it then check in.

Chapter Fourteen

Not long after sitting down Charlie came in and sat down across from me.

He leaned over the table and looked at me closely. "Are you Ok now?" he asked.

"I know I've been a little strange lately but, Yes I'm fine now, I found out what was happening and why I was feeling so funny about the painting you hung up over there." I said trying not to laugh.

"Oh? Well are you going to let me in on what was happening? Or do I have to find a real bright light?" he said fighting a smile.

"Ok, well the painting you have hanging over there was painted by my lost twin. I didn't know I had a twin till all this went down. I was feeling so funny because I was picking up on Anna, my twin's feelings about the painting. Oh, by the way, Anna is the one that just sold some of her other paintings for over three million dollars, so this one is worth even more money because this one was her first painting offered to the public." I explained.

"You mean, the painting I have over there is worth over a ah mil million duh dollars?" he stammered, while falling back into the chair.

"Yes and the artist is my sister. Pretty cool huh?" I said proudly.

"Well sister or not, you had better clock in." he said with a big Cheshire cat grin.

Swallowing the last of my soda I checked in and got to the front. The day was going as usual. We have a lot of regular customers that come in everyday and order the same thing almost every time. Having time off was like having a mini vacation.

I had just placed a customer's order on the table when I heard, "Ahh, there is the painting I have heard so much about"

I looked toward the door. The sun was streaming through the door just right to keep me seeing who was talking. I could only see a tall, slender figure of a man, wearing what looked like a suit.

He walked closer to me and I was able to get a better look at him. I got the strangest feeling that I knew him. He looked like he was in his late thirty's. What looked to be a suit, turned out to be a lab smock, except it was covered in splats and dribbles of paint.

Standing there, I caught myself staring, *'Humm, where have I seen him before? Oh yeah he was in a drawing that Anna showed to me the other night. In my dream we were standing in an art studio. She said he was her art teacher, Master uh....., oh man. What was his name?'"* I asked myself.

Charlie came out of his office to greet the man, who was starting to sit at a table facing the painting.

"Hello, I am Charlie Hanson, the proud owner of this establishment. I see you are enjoying our painting." he said putting his hand out offering to shake hands.

"Yes, this is the greatest piece of art work I have ever seen. The brush strokes, the blending of the colors, the way it presents itself to the viewer." he went on while looking at Anna's artwork. "Oh, I am Sorry, where are my manners? I am Master Bastrono, an artist and teacher." he said, while shaking hands with Charlie, he proceeded to sit down at a table close to the front door, so as to see the whole painting.

"Please, you must see the full effect of this painting." Charlie said while gesturing for Master Bastrono to follow him.

Master Bastrono got up and walked closer to the painting, following Charlie.

"Oh My! Oh Goodness!" Master Bastrono said almost shouting in excitement. "It is a different painting all together, it changed. How Wonderful. How extraordinary indeed." he continued.

"The artist that painted this painting is the same as the one that painted "Two Hands Shaking", "Butterfly Trees". This one didn't have a name till Rita named it "Fairy's Delight." Charlie said, motioning for me to come over and join in the conversation. "This is Rita, Anna May Stolks' sister, the artist of this and the other paintings I mentioned." Charlie continued.

"Rita this is Master Bastrono, he is an artist and teacher." Charlie said as I held out my hand to shake hands. Instead Master Bastrono bowed to me.

"Honored I am sure." Master Bastrono said. "So it is your sister that created this wonderful painting?" he continued.

"Yes, my twin sister. That is a story in itself. I didn't know I had a sister till a few days ago. These last few weeks has been a whirlwind." I said, feeling a little shy.

Then it hit me, like a ton of bricks, as

the old saying goes. I just remembered, "*I wasn't to meet Master Bastrono for four more years. Oh No, what is this going to do to Anna's time when she gets back.*" I thought. "*I really need to talk to Anna.*"

"Here is my card Miss Rita, if you have even half the talent of your sister, I would love to teach you what I know." Master Bastrono said as I took his business card.

"Thank you Master Bastrono, I really must get back to our customers." I said, franticly searching my pockets for Anna's phone number.

"Yes, you do that Rita" Charlie said joining in the conversation again.

I took care of the few customers that had come in after Master Bastrono had arrived, and then I went to the back to search the pockets of my jacket. "Jiminy jumping Christmas! It's not here either" I thought out loud.

"What's not here?" Jimmy asked

while standing near the dish rack.

"Oh, I was just looking for a phone number I thought I had." I said, looking up to see Jimmy. "Are the dishes caught up? Because we needed the large dinner plates a few customers ago." I asked.

"Oh sure, they are waiting on the end of the dish drain for you. See I remember when you tell me what you need." he said laughing. "I like playing like I don't hear, sometimes it gets me an extra break if Charlie doesn't know I hear everything, so shhhhh!" he added with a chuckle.

"Ok Jimmy, you can be such a character sometimes, but I guess that is what makes it fun to work here." I said, joining in with the laughter.

"I need to call Nell real quick. Oh, well never mind, if she had the number I need, it would be at her house and she's at work right now." I said, thinking out loud again.

"You're doing it again, Rita." Jimmy

said while rolling his eyes.

"Doing what?" I asked.

"Thinking out loud" he said.

Chapter Fifteen

"Oh yeah, sorry." I said franticly trying to think of a way to get in touch with Anna before she left. She was to leave in about thirty-eight hours.

The day went on and I was waiting for George to come in for his drink. He always took a ten minute coffee or soda break in the late afternoon when I was ready to go home.

"Hi George, I think you are running a little late today. Aren't you"" I said looking up at the clock over the door.

"Nope, your clock is a little fast." he said, as he sat down with a pleased smile on one of the stools.

"Shhhh, don't tell Charlie." I said laughing.

"Oh, OK, mumms the word." he said

joining me in laughter.

We both knew that Charlie was standing right behind me, with his hands on his hips, trying to look very stern and grumpy.

I looked behind me at Charlie and, we all started laughing even more.

"Well it's been a long day, both of you get out of here and leave me in pieces." said Charlie laughing even harder.

"Well! I guess we know when we aren't wanted anymore." I said as George and I stood up to go to the bus.

"Yeah, I guess we do." said George and we laughed all the way to the bus.

"Well it sounds like you had a good day, George." I said.

"Oh I did, I really did. You know that raise I got, helped me to be able to keep a smile on my face even with some of the rude people I pick up farther downtown." he said with a slight giggle.

"I am glad it helped to make your

day. Good I see Nell; I need to talk to her. Later George." I said waving to get Nell's attention.

"Hi Nell." I said getting close to her. Gee the bus is crowded again tonight." I said as I sat down.

"So what is new?" asked Nell.

"Well let me see, where was I when I left you this morning?" I said trying to remember.

"You had just told me about Anna's back operation." she reminded me.

"Oh yeah. Well she will be going back in about 30 hours from now. She showed me a drawing of herself and the art teacher that had taught her how to paint. She said I would find him in San Francisco, California in about four years. Well guess who showed up at the Rooster today?" I said trying to keep my voice down.

"You're kidding! Well what is that going to affect Anna's life?" Nell asked looking around to see who was listening.

"I don't know, I got away from him as fast as I could, but he gave me his business card and hinted he wanted to teach me how to paint like Anna." I said.

"Well, I think you better talk to Anna as soon as you can, before she leaves." Nell suggested.

"I think you're right. I plan to call as soon as I get home." I said.

"Yeah, well you had better call me after that and let me know what she says." said Nell with almost a whisper.

"Deal" I said as we shook hands on it.

Looking up I could see we were getting close to my stop. "I will call you soon." I said getting up and making my way to the back door of the bus.

"Bye George and thanks, Bye Nell." I said as I got off the bus.

"Ahh Anna. How was your day? Mine was pretty weird." I said picking her up and carrying her upstairs to our apartment.

"Good, home once again," I said kicking off my shoes and tossing my jacket on the couch.

Anna ran for the kitchen right off. "What is this? Hungry so soon, didn't do any hunting today? Ok, Ok, I will get you something to eat." I said opening up the refrigerator. "Do you want cat food or milk?" I asked, waiting for her to let me know. I put the cat food on one side of the refrigerator and the milk on the other. Anna would stand up on her hind legs and place her paw in front of the one she wanted. She had learned this when she was a very young kitten. "Ok, milk it is." I said taking it out and pouring it into her bowl near the stove.

"Now, I really must find my other self's phone number," I said.

Anna looked up at me and cocked her head a little to one side and meowed. "Oh I know it is confusing to you. I promise I will explain things to you a little later." I said, walking out of the room to find Anna's phone number.

It was just where I thought it might be, in my other jacket pocket along with my new bus pass. "Good now I can make the call." I said under my breath.

Picking up the phone I dialed Anna's number. "Hello Anna?"

"Yes?" she said.

"This is Rita, I had something happen at work today, I thought you may need to know about." I started to explain about Master Bastrono.

As I explained what had happened and what I did, it was almost like I could hear her thinking. "What kind of a difference will that make for you in your time" I asked.

"I'm not real sure but it lets me know that minor things in the past do change. I guess you could take a few lessons here and there from him, but don't make any paintings like I have done, and if you do, don't let anyone know for about ten years. It just seems real strange that he showed up at your work place four years sooner than you were to find him." said Anna. "But you know, come to think about it, I take back what I just said...I am selling the paintings now, not four years from now." She said. "It is me that was off a few years on my timing." she added.

"Well not to worry too much about me learning to paint. I have to save enough money for all the supplies first. That will take me a while to save that much." I said with a laugh. "Can I be there when you leave and watch you go" I asked.

"If you are not working at the time," then she paused for a moment. "Let me think, I am to leave tomorrow evening about eight PM. Sure, if you want to watch, I don't see a problem with that." she added.

"So where are you leaving from?" I asked.

"Meet James and me at 2305 States St, upstairs room 208. It's a room we rent just for this kind of purpose. This way there is no one looking for us and interrupting the process. Our agency here, over sees to all the arrangements." Anna explained.

"Ok, I'll be there." I said.

"Oh better yet, how about I have James bring me by your place and we will all go together to States Street? How does that sound?" she asked.

"That sounds great! Thanks. See you tomorrow night." I said. "Good night"

"Good night Rita and thanks for the heads up." Anna said before hanging up.

My Anna had finished her milk and was wrapping herself around my legs now. Meowing as she walked around in circles. I knew she was hungry.

"Let me get in the kitchen and get us something to eat. Ok baby girl?" I said.

Darting out in front of me Anna jumped on to one of the kitchen chairs that was sitting away from the table, and sat there waiting on me to get her something to eat. She cocked her head and meowed a few times to let me know I was taking too long.

"Well you know, I could just fix this for me and give you cat food. But better yet you have something special in the frig." I said while stroking her head. She laid down on the chair and waited patiently.

"I'm not sure what Mandy boxed up for you last night." I said opening the box. "It looks like steak cut into small bite size pieces with gravy dribbled over it." I added.

I took her dinner and mine to the living room where we ate while watching a little TV. Then off to bed we went. I was tired and I knew morning would come quicker that I wanted it to. Having the few extra days off over the last few weeks like I did, had gotten me out of the early to rise mode and had made me a little lazy.

Before I knew it, the early morning sun was glaring through my window and warming my face. Anna just laid there on her pillow soaking it all in. "Boy a cats' life,

Anna you have it so good. There are days I wish I could trade you places. Come on girl, let's go get something to eat." I urged Anna to get up.

Bouncing onto the floor, Anna raced me to the kitchen, turned around and meowed at me trying to be cute. "Yes your cute, Anna, And I will make you something special this morning." I told her as she jumped on to the chair again.

"We have a few pieces of lunch meat left. I think I will cook them up for us. How does that sound?" I asked looking over at Anna.

She was sitting quietly on the chair washing herself.

"Oh, getting ready for breakfast are you?" I asked with a giggle.

She looked up and gave a curious "meow."

"Your breakfast is almost finished, but I'm going to have a couple of eggs and toast with mine." I said.

Putting the meat on her plate and pouring milk into her saucer, was enough for her to give me a long meow with a little purring at the end.

"You are very welcome." I said giving her a few strokes. "You are such a good little friend." I added.

I finished cooking my breakfast and sat down to eat. Anna had finished eating and was wrapping around the chair legs and mine.

"Today is my catch-up day Anna, and you know what that means; cleaning house, washing the clothes at Mama Duffy's Laundry-mat around the corner." I explained.

Anna looked at me, curled her tail and meowed as if to say she knew exactly what I was saying. She enjoyed going with me on wash day. Mama Duffy has a little dog and they seem to love playing chase.

"First I need to call Nell and tell her what Anna said." I said looking over at her.

She was sitting there with her head tilted to one side as if to say "What? I'm right here."

I had to laugh, "The other Anna." I explained

She gave me a quick "Meow" put her tail in the air and trotted off to the bedroom.

After getting off the phone, I gathered up the laundry and, the soap and carried it all to the door.

I heard a faint meow coming from the bedroom. It was one of those meows' that sounds like, "help".

Chapter Sixteen

Putting the basket down, I went back to the bedroom. I could hear Anna meowing but couldn't tell where the meows were coming from. After looking in and under everything in the bedroom and bathroom I opened the closet door.

There she sat looking at me as if to say "it took you long enough." She gave a couple of meows and pranced out of the closet and headed straight to the front door.

"Anna, how did you get shut up in the closet?" I asked following her to the front door

She gave another meow and just sat on the basket of clothes.

"Oh!" I laughed; you must have been in the closet when I closed the door after getting the laundry basket. You know maybe I should put the basket in the bathroom and not behind the closet door. I'll think about that later. Right now we need to go wash my clothes." I said laughing quietly to myself while opening the front door.

Anna jumped off the basket and was the first one out of the door. Down the stairs she went as if in a race.

Anna was as good as any dog when it came to going for walks with me to the market or the laundry-mat. She tagged along anytime I left the house except when I placed her on the steps, when I had to go to work. It was as if she knew the difference.

Anna seemed to love wash day. She would curl up in one of the chairs near a dryer asleep after playing with Jessy, her little doggy friend. We would take a short break for lunch and then she would walk with me to Johnson's Market. She would sit outside by the door and wait for me. She knew she was going to eat when I went to the market.

When I came out this time I didn't see Anna right off. Someone had tied their big dog near the front door. I found Anna perched on he shelf above the fruit crate in front of the store.

I gathered up Anna in one arm and carried the food in the other back to Mama's laundry-mat, where we ate lunch, finished the clothes and walked back to our apartment.

I finished all my chores for the day but it seemed that time had gone by fast. It wasn't long before I needed to get ready to meet Anna. James and Anna were to pick me up in about an hour.

As I made dinner for my Anna and myself, she sat and watched from her favorite kitchen chair.

"I'm going out for a little while tonight, so you will need to be a good kitty and entertain yourself. I'll leave the TV on for you." I explained

Putting her dinner in her dish, I said, "Come on your dinner is ready. We are having macaroni and cheese with slices of hotdog mixed in just the way you like it. After we eat, I have to do the dishes and get dressed. James will be here in a little while." I added.

I had just finished pulling my hair back when there was a knock at the door. Anna ran to the door as if she could answer it.

As I opened the door, Anna meowed as if to say hello.

"Well, Hello Anna!" said James with a big smile. He stooped down and petted her.

"Hi James." I said with a smile.

"Are you ready to go?" he asked

"Yes," I said looking down at Anna, who was wrapping herself around my legs. "Now you be a good girl and I will be back in a little while."

I placed her on the couch, grabbed my jacket from off the nearby chair, locked and closed the door.

"Are we going to the Clair Mont?" I asked, waiting for the answer as we walked out onto the street.

"No, we're going to a place on States Street. Remember?" James said looking at me questioningly.

"Oh that's right. This whole thing has been so exciting and strange, it's like being in a dream at times." I said, while getting into the limo.

James closed my door, went around and got in.

"So where is Anna? I thought she was coming with you to get me," I asked feeling puzzled.

"No, she needed to take care of a few last minute things before she left, so she went on ahead. We will meet her there." he explained.

"So have you time traveled before,

James?" I asked.

"Only once so far." he said with a smile as he started the engine.

"So this is your first time? What do you think about it?" I asked curiously.

"Rita! Slow Down." he laughed. "Yes this is my first time and I sort of like it, especially the part of being young again." he said while paying attention to the road.

"So what happens if you were to get hurt or sick while you are time traveling? Anything?" I asked.

"The same thing that would happen if this was in my own time period." he answered as if to think about it a few seconds. "Well, here we are." he added.

"Already? I thought it would have taken longer." I said, as he turned off the engine.

"Anna is on the second floor waiting for us." James said, opening the door.

We walked in the front doors of the apartment house and James led me to the stairwell.

"We'll walk up, that way there are fewer people to see us here. The time checkers rent the apartment on a regular basis, that way it's ready for all of us." he explained on our way up the stairs.

After James knocked twice and then scratched the door, we heard a voice from inside. "Who is it?" James knocked once scratched and the knocked again.

The door opened and a young looking but white haired woman stood in the doorway. She looked at both of us then motioned for us to enter.

"Hi Steffy, this is Rita, Anna May's younger self. Anna requested for her to be able to witness the travel back." James explained

"Oh yes, Anna mentioned that to me yesterday on the phone. Anna is in the next room being prepared for the trip." she said pointing to a door on her left.

I started to ask, but she answered my

question before I could ask it. "Yes, it's ok for you to go in and visit while she gets ready to travel." she said with a smile.

I walked slowly toward the door, wondering how it was that she knew what I was going to ask. Then it dawned on me, in her time line I may have already asked the question.

Opening the door, there stood Anna in a light metallic jumper suit with a high collar that zipped up the front. "Rita, want to see a little of the future?" she asked looking up from snapping her front pockets shut. "Since there have been others who have been where you are standing now 'situation wise', I mean, who wanted to - there is a device that helps to link the two (present and future self) together...this way the present self can see the future the way it was before the time traveler came to the past." she explained.

"Really, for real, I can see your time line?" I asked eagerly. "Yes! Please!" I answered fast before anyone could think and say no.

"Okay, well, I need you to sit down over there in that large chair." Anna said pointing to a large metallic chair with a metal step joined to it. It reminded me of a dentist chair except it was metal.

Walking towards it she handed me a cushion, "here this will make it easier to sit still." she said with a smile while she sat down in the other one next to me.

Steffy walked in holding what looked to be two helmets with a lot of wires running from
one to the other. Placing the one helmet on my head, she said, "Not to worry dear, this won't hurt at all. The whole thing will seem like a vivid dream to you. But you will get a chance to see how Anna lives in her time line-your future. But I imagine some of that will be changed for the better now since Anna has the financing she needed to do other things." she continued.

"That's right a few things **will** change, and hopefully for the better." chimed in Anna with a giggle.

"Okay, both of you sit very still. Anna, I am starting the count down so start thinking about what you want Rita to see. She will only see what you think of, so think and see it in your mind as clear as you can." Steffy explained.

"Now Rita, close your eyes and I am going to give you a very small shot to just relax you, so you can see what Anna wants to show you more clearly" She explained "Just a small poke, and then just take a few long deep breaths to relax. Lay back as if to take a short nap. It will only relax you. You will still know everything that is happening around you and can react if needed. But if you do, it will bring you out of the dream like state of seeing. Do you understand?" she asked as she stuck me with a very small, fine pointed needle.

"Yes," I said, not wanting to exert

very much energy to answer.

Chapter Seventeen

In my mind, I seemed to be walking down a country lane with a few maple trees scatted among evergreens. There were nice homes with large yards and lots of flowers. It was peaceful, and looked like it should have been on a picture postcard.

I could hear Anna's voice speaking to me softly. She was letting me know what I was seeing and where I was.

"This is the street where I live. My house is just up the lane about another block. It will be on the right hand side and it is the one with the light blue fence around the front part of the house. I have a small dog now.

I lost Anna, our cat, about thirty-six years ago. Sparky is a very nice little dog. He is from one of my present friends." Anna spoke softly.

I had to smile when I saw Sparky. He was a cute little dog with bright black eyes and very energetic. He had short wavy hair of multi colored splotches and very loving. He greeted me at the gate and bounced alongside me as we walked into the house.

Stepping into the house I found myself in a very well kept home. Everything seemed peaceful and joyful. Next I found myself in the kitchen, feeding Sparky and then I was in an art studio. I had paintings on the walls, leaning up against all of the furniture in the room. Some of them looked a lot like the ones Anna had just painted here, but different. Most of them were painting that had two pictures in them, like the one hanging in The Rooster Cafe. But for some reason she had never tried to sell any of them.

The thought was that people weren't ready for them. By going back in time, she had a chance to get the future ready for this kind of artwork. Of this I was sure, after all she had sold a few for a lot of money.

Here in her time, people were given work to do, for which they were suited for and all of their physical needs were taken care of. They worked on their jobs for six hour a days, four days on and then two days off to take care of their hobbies or self-explorations and expressions. They could do anything they wanted to do as long as it didn't get in the way of others and they had the finances to do it.

There aren't many crimes because everyone was given the same treatment. The elected officials didn't live, earn or get any extra privileges than any other common person. If or when someone did decide they were better than others and stole something or worst, they were severally dealt with.

Anna wanted to travel to the past to set up a desire for her kind of artwork and for this she had to borrow from the state. This kind of a loan needed to be paid back within a few months of her coming back. Fortunately this wasn't going to be a problem, because of the money she had from the sales of her paintings. It was placed into an account for her and was waiting for her in her present time and it included the interest for the years it sat in the account.

The skies were so blue and clear. All of the energy used was powered by wind, water and solar. They now had ways of storing this power, so when it was stormy or something else, there was plenty of power to run whatever they needed.

People seemed happy. They worked on jobs they liked, no one had to work at a job they didn't like and because of this all areas of production were of great quality. The world was united, it was all one people. Yes there were differences in beliefs and customs, but nothing was forced on anyone else.

"Ok Rita," Steffi's voice came into my dream softly. "It is time to wake up, Anna has to get ready to leave and you said you wanted to see her off."

"Yes, I do" I said opening my eyes.

"Anna, is what you showed me all true?" I asked looking her straight in the eyes.

"Yes Rita, it is. We all live a good life. My job is or was to paint pictures for businesses and peoples' homes. That is what I do and in exchange for my art work, I am given housing, all the food I can eat, transportation, entertainment, health and medical, and time to work my own art to sell for cash or barter. Oh yes, and I am given a vacation each year at one of the many wonderful resorts. It's great! I enjoy my life. Well it's time for me to return." she said giving me a hug and then climbing into what looked a little like an egg shell.

Steffy walked over and shut the capsule door. Then there was a flash of light, the door opened and Anna was gone.

"Is that all there is to it?" I asked.

"Yes, that is all there is to it. The person climbs inside; we set the controls and send them where ever they were preset to go." Steffy said with a smile as James walked into the room.

"Ready for me Steffy?" asked James.

"Hi Rita, so did you get a chance to see a little of the future?" he asked as he finished snapping the pocket of his metallic jump suit.

"Yes I did and right now it looks good. That is, what I had a chance to see of it." I said, waiting to see what he was going to do next.

James walked over, sat down in the capsule. Sticking his thumb up, he said "Steffy! Ready on this end."

"Okay James, shut the door, I'm ready here." she said.

"Bye Rita, nice meeting you, maybe I'll see you again in the future," then he laughed, "Of course I will, in just a few minutes." then he laughed even more.

"Later" he said as he shutting the capsule door. And with a flash of light it was all done as if it was an everyday thing.

Walking over to me, Steffy placed her hand on my shoulder. "Now you understand you can never tell anyone anything you saw or heard here tonight."

"Yes, I understand that, like anyone would ever believe me any way." I said laughing.

"Yes, I think you are right about that." replied Steffy as she joined me in laughter. I will have Jack drive you back to your house. He is one of our local time people, who is stationed in this time.

"Hi Rita," said Jack stretching out his hand in the gesture of a handshake.

"Hi Jack, glad to meet you." I said as we started for the door. Turning around I wanted to say good-bye to Steffy, but she was nowhere to be found. "What happened to Steffy?" I asked looking at Jack.

"Oh she went back to the same time

as Anna and James. She was from their time.
We always have a time tech travel along
with anyone that is time traveling. That way
they can help get this set up for them. You
see those of us who stay and manage things
at this end, have no idea how the machines
work. We have a small machine that we can
send and receive messages on, but that is
the most we are taught. That way if anyone
here decided to run and hide in a different
time, there wouldn't be anyone here they
could force to help them. No one in our
group could help. Taking care of the
apartment and keeping the equipment safe
is my job. I was placed here for that reason"
he explained as we walked down the stairs
to the limo.

"So Jack? What time are you from
and how do you stay here more than three
months?" I asked, moving forward in my
seat and looking in the rear view mirror.

"Oh Rita." James said "You are full of
questions" he said with a chuckle. "Well I

am from about 32 years from now and one of the time techs checks in with me every few months and gives me the treatment I need to stay here and do my job." he explained. "If I decided I wanted to go back to my time, one of the time techs would have to come and get me." He continued.

"So how old are you really?" I asked

Laughing he said "Well at the end of this month I will be fifty-nine years young."

"Young is right. You don't look like you should be any older than thirty years." I said joining him in the laughter.

After getting home I had a lot to think about. And I figured it would take a while. What a whirl wind of a time. *'Time'* I had to laugh. That word had a whole new meaning.

Walking up the stairs my mind was still spinning from all that had just happened. As I found myself in front of my door, I thought *'I guess I was on auto pilot. I got home without much thought about it."*

Opening the front door, I saw Anna was sitting there waiting to greet me. She meowed as if to ask how things went.

I sat on the edge of the bed and explained everything that had happened while getting dressed for bed. Anna sat beside me giving a little meow, just in the right spots as if she understood everything I was telling her.

"You're such a good listener." I said giving her a few strokes. "Let's go to bed, it's been a long day." I added.

With a quickness she was curled up on her pillow, waiting for me to turn off my bedside lamp.

Good Night Anna." I said.

"Meow" came her response.

Chapter Eighteen

Morning came with the sun trying to shine between the rain clouds.

"Looks like it may rain today Anna." I said, looking at her on our way to the kitchen.

Anna seemed to be right on cue. We both finished breakfast fairly fast. I had a lot of things to do before I could go see Nell.

I cleaned the kitchen as quick as I could, and then started on the rest of the house.

"Anna, leave your toys in the box. I have to go to Nell's in a little while, so don't be dragging out your toys." I scolded her after she had already dragged three out onto the floor near her box.

She tilted her head and dragged out her favorite mouse anyway.

"Okay, Anna but only the one toy, leave the rest of them alone." I said, giving her my serious look while putting the other three back in her box.

With a meow she took her mouse and trotted off towards the bedroom. I found her on the bed playing when I went in to make the bed.

"Okay Anna, time to go play somewhere else, I need to make our bed." I explained. But she was in one of her playful moods. Every time I started to straighten the covers, she got under them and tried to catch my hands. This went on for a while. I have to admit I was having as much fun as she was.

"Okay Anna, I really need to get the bed made. Today is Nell's day off and she is expecting me to come over. She wants me to tell her everything that happened yesterday with Anna." I explained while Anna tilled her head to look at me sideways. I had to laugh. "My other self, Anna" I added. "She went forward to her own time. She went home last night."

Anna meowed, letting me know she understood and jumped off the bed carrying her mouse with her.

"Oh my goodness, it's almost three o'clock. I really have to go now!" I said excitedly while dumping cat food into Anna's bowl. "I will make us something better to eat when I get back home." I added while Anna looked on. "I need to be at Nell's house in a few minutes. You be a good girl and I'll be back as soon as I can." I said while turned on the TV, Anna took her mouse and jumped onto the couch as I walked out the door and locked it behind me.

As I hurried towards Nell's house it started to sprinkle very lightly, then as I reached her steps it started to sprinkle heavier. As I reached out to ring the doorbell it started to rain harder.

"Oh! hi Rita," said Nell as she opened

the door. "You surprised me; I was waiting on you to call. I thought maybe something had come up. I was starting to think about food." She continued with a big smile and a giggle.

"Oh?, Well I can always come back later," I said turning around as if to leave, then turning back around as we both started to laugh.

"Oh you, come on in, I have an early dinner ready to go on the table. You want to join me?" asked Nell.

"Sure, don't mind if I do." I answered quickly. "I came straight over after getting things set up at my apartment."

"I didn't make anything fancy, just some homemade soup and French bread." Nell informed me on our way to the kitchen.

"That sounds good to me. Soup is good stuff." I said smiling.

"Okay, so out with it. What happened last night?" she blurted out in excitement.

"Oh. Not too much." I said teasingly,

and then I explained every detail I thought was safe to tell as we ate lunch.

"Wow, that is a lot of information." she said.

"You're telling me, and I was in the middle of it all. But you know you can't tell anyone anything about what I said here today. Right?" I said.

"Yes of course. People would think I was crazy anyway." she said laughing. "I wonder how many changes this trip will make in Anna's life." Nell said looking toward the ceiling. "and I wonder if we will see her again." she added looking back at me.

"I have no idea, but I hope it doesn't change much. I mean finances were the only thing she really wanted to change." I informed Nell.

Both of us took a deep breath and reclined in our chairs and laid there quietly, looking at the ceiling for what seemed a long time.

"Wow!, What a whirl wind!" Nell said breaking the silence and making me jump a little.

"Well, that was a jolt." I said laughing. "I must have really been out there wondering around."

"Oh you mean when I broke the silence?" Nell questioned.

"Yeah, you didn't see me jump?" I asked starting to laugh.

"I guess I wasn't paying that much attention." she said joining me in laughter. "Well, I guess if this trip messed up anything important, she can come back and fix it." Nell added.

"I don't know, I remember seeing an old movie about a time traveler who had made a mess of things and the more he came back to fix one thing, something else got messed up. Till the end when he just gave up trying and he stopped long enough to figure out how to fix things without traveling back in time." I said looking over at Nell. "And in another one, the changes just made a different timeline. And his consciousness decided which time he would experience at that moment.   This traveler had gone back to document what happened in a war and when he came back into his time it had changed a few things. While he was gone, the scientist of his time found out that nothing major really gets changed in their own time. But it may have been changed in the traveler's timeline. The traveler had creates another timeline. I have often wondered about that. I mean we have the chance to change our future at any point with just one action or another. So I really wonder if there are other timelines or other realities and we only see the one we are conscious of and that is our reality at that moment." I said, looking over at Nell.

"Well, we may never know, at least not for a very long time." she said.

"Wow, is it really that late?" I asked, looking over at Nell's wall clock.

"Yeah, it looks that way." Nell said standing up to see her clock better.

"I had better get going, Anna will be wondering what happened to me." I said getting up and heading for the front door. "See you on the bus tomorrow." I added.

"Ok, I'll see you then." Nell said waving to me as I walked down the street toward my place.

Arriving home, I found Anna sleeping on the couch with the TV remote at the edge of one paw. The station had been changed and there was a talk show on about quantum physics. I listened for a while before Anna woke up and found me sitting next to her.

"Hey baby girl, since when did you like listening to talk shows?" I said in a quiet voice while stroking her on the back.

She gave me a meow as she got up with a long stretch and trotted off to the kitchen.

"I'll be there is a little while, you got

me interested in what they are talking about." I said as she meowed again. "I will fix you something during the next commercial." I answered.

I sat and listened while the two scientists bounced around the idea of time travel and alternate timelines. Nell and I had almost the same conversation but these two were scientists and should know more than the two of us. I found myself wanting to remember as much as I could so I could tell Nell in the morning.

When the commercial came on I hurried into the kitchen and put one of the left over franks into the microwave, just long enough to take the chill off. Put it into Anna's bowl just as the program came back on. "There you go girl, I really need to hear what these two are talking about." I said walking back into the living room.

After watching for a while longer, my eyes got the best of me and I found I was falling asleep while trying to listen. I looked at the clock and I had been sitting there for over three hours. I vaguely remember hearing Anna meow as she went by on her way to the bedroom.

I got in the bed and fell fast asleep into a dream about time travel of all things.

Morning came fast and I had to really rush to make it to the bus stop in time to catch George.

"Hi George, what a day, and the rush is starting already." I said laughing as George punched two hole in my bus pass.

I spotted Nell toward the back of the bus and waved to her on my way back to her.

We talked all the way to my stop and I told her about what had happened when I got home and about the scientist I had tried to listen to.

When I got to work, I checked everything out to make sure it was all the same as it was when I got off work last. *"Yep, the painting is still here and everyone that was working that day is here.*" I thought as I looked around.

Nell and I talked off and on about ideas of timelines, different realities and time travel for the next few months. Everything seemed to be going along smoothly, pretty much the way it had before Charlie had bought the painting. Well, except for more business. Then one morning Master Bastrono walked in and ordered breakfast. He sat and studied the painting while eating. I was busy cleaning a few tables, getting ready for the next group of people that usually came in for a later breakfast or early lunch, when he grabbed my hand as I walked by with a tray full of dishes.

"We need to talk, you and I." he said looking straight into my eyes.

This gave me the weirdest feeling.

"When is your lunch break?" he asked with a smile.

Looking at my watch, I said "In about

fifteen minutes."

"Good please come back and sit with me at that time." he said politely.

I went about my work and set up so it would be easy to take a few minutes longer on my break. I just had a feeling, that what he had to say was going to be important.

"Sandy! I'm taking lunch before the next rush." I informed her.

She nodded and went back to stacking the dishes.

Grabbing myself a sandwich and soda I went over to Master Bastrono's table.

"So what do you need to talk to me about?" I asked, sitting down across from him.

"You see that painting hanging on that wall?" he said while pointing to the painting that Anna had painted.

"Yes? What about it?" I asked, wondering where this conversation was going.

"I want to talk to you about this

painting of your sister's." he said drawing out the "your sister's" with a wink. "I know all about it" he said. "I am also a traveler, but from a different time." he continued in almost a whisper.

"I was told I wouldn't meet you for four years yet. But I met you showed up now." I said feeling confused.

"Oh not to worry, where I am from this conversation has already been and I will explain all this to you later." he said with a chuckle.

"Confused yet?" he asked, looking at me with a smile. "Well I explained to Anna that the paintings needed to be painted and sold now while people are in need of them, not later. This will also help her not to have to worry about money in the future. Understand a little now?" he asked with a smile.

"Yes, I think I understand what you are saying." I said still not really clear on what was happening, or what it had to do with me.

"Well then, let me teach you a few things about painting in the next few weeks." he offered.

"But don't I need to go to San Francisco first, like Anna did?" I asked.

"Not really, you can skip that part, I can show you everything you learned there." he said with a smile. "So can we start this week end?" he asked.

"I don't have anything to paint or draw with." I said.

"That's fine, I will bring everything you will need to start out." he offered.

"Well, if you think everything will stay the same or be even better for the future." I said, still trying to sort out this whirl wind.

"I will be at your apartment this Saturday morning about ten AM." he said getting up from the table and looking at his watch.

"Okay." I said softly as he walked

away. I just sat there trying to sort out everything he had said.

Luckily the rest of the day went without incident and quitting time seem to come quickly.

I caught the bus and said hi to George as usual and found Nell sitting on the back seat. As soon as I sat down and she started asking questions. She could tell by looking at me that something strange had happened.

I explained the whole conversation I had had with Master Bastrono, to Nell.

"So are you going to take the lessons from him now or are you going to try and wait the four years?" she asked giving me this curious look.

"Well it does seem logical, that if I learned how to paint the paintings now and was able to sell them, then I wouldn't have to come back and sell them later in my life." I said trying to sort it all out.

"Ok, but what is that going to do with the painting that Anna just painted?" Nell ask.

"Good question," I said becoming even more confused. "I think we have a lot of thinking to do between now and Saturday morning." I said looking over at Nell with a smile.

On Saturday I had just finished washing the morning dishes when I heard a knock on my door.

Drying my hands I opened the front door. Master Bastrono almost pushed his way past me as if he was in a hurry. His arms were full of all the supplies we would need to paint.

"Close the door, close the door quickly" he urged, trying not to sound frantic.

"What is the problem?" I asked.

"Nothing for you to be alarmed about" he said as he put all the supplies down in a corner of the living room.

"I'm not too sure about that. This whole deal seems very strange to me. Anna said I would meet you in four years and here you are now and you almost ran over me just now getting through the door." I said really concerned.

Chapter Nineteen

"I thought I spotted another traveler down the hallway of your building." he said.

"So, what does that have to do with you? And how can you tell if that person is a traveler?" I asked.

"Ok, Ok." he said as he took off his coat. "All travelers are given a special pair of contacts that enables us to see the glow that shows around fellow travelers. Before we are given the ok to travel we are given a shot that gives our skin a special glow that can only be seen with the contacts." he said pointing to his eyes. "That way we don't get the people we are visiting mixed up with the travelers. Like when I came back this time. That is how I could keep you and Anna straight." he explained.

Just then my Anna came walking into the room meowing. She looked at him and I noticed her hair stand up.

"He wasn't talking about you baby girl." I said as I picked her up and stroked her back.

"Your cat is named Anna?" he asked with a smile.

"Yes, and don't change the subject." I said. "Did you talk to Anna about all this before she left?" I prodded.

"Well, sort of." he replied.

"What do you mean sort of?" I asked, becoming even more concerned. My thoughts flashed back to the envelope that Anna had given me and said "do not to open" and pointed to a coded date on the outside. *When I told her about her teacher showing up and his idea at the time, she seem to think it might work out if I only took a few lessons. But his actions just now mixed with Anna's have me a little uneasy.*

"Let me get you something to drink

while you explain about the arrangement you made with Anna and we will see where we go from there." I said. "I have milk, water, tea and a soda. What would you like?" I asked.

"Some water would be nice." he said as he joined me in the kitchen. "Well, I caught up with Anna the day before she was to go back and I explained that I could teach her, uh, I mean you, in this time and that way it would improve her life in the future. Besides people are interested in her way of paintings now, and I would like to see that interest continues. This way she really wouldn't have to come back to sell them, but maybe just to visit, if she wanted to." he explained. "Just make sure that you keep most of the money you get, tied it up in gold or the stock tip she gave you." he continued.

'Hummm, that last part made me a little more uneasy. After all how would he have known about the envelope, or what may be in it.

But again

they had managed to mess with my birth

certificate before all this started.' I thought.

"I'll be right back. Stay right there.
Ok?" I instructed.

"Ok." he said while sipping his
water.

I walked into my bedroom and closed
the door. I had put the envelope in my top
drawer where I kept all my important
papers, but this time I had sealed it in
another envelope then put it in with my
photos. As I opened the drawer I could tell
things had been moved. I opened the box of
photo and noticed they had been moved
around too! I took out the envelope I had
sealed Anna's message envelope in. When I
opened it I could tell it had been messed
with. It had been put back in the envelope
upside down. Now the question was, had
someone changed just the outside envelope
or the contents that Ann had given me? And
if they had, what could I do about it? It

wasn't like I could just give her a call and ask a question. I gently lifted the right folded crease of the envelope edge to see if the small pin point I had placed on it was still there. "Aw" I sighed. *'It was still there it seemed that they had nosed around but hadn't changed anything else,'* as I closed my drawer, Anna meowed at the bedroom door.

"Ok, I'm coming." I said as I hurried and flushed the toilet.

I opened the bedroom door and there sat Anna waiting for me to come and give her some milk. "Ok, let's go get you something to drink." I said as she followed me to the kitchen.

"Master Bastrono, are you saying that the other you is still in San Francisco right now?" I asked as I sat down with a glass of water after taking care of Anna.

"No, he is in India for another year." he said with a smile.

"So if I was to learn how to paint like now instead of later, at the normal four years it will make it easier on me in the future?" I asked.

"Well, that is the idea. You see, you only wanted to come back now to be able to sell some of your work, so you would have enough funds to be able to go and experience some of the things you will be interested in, in your future." he explained.

"That makes sense, but I am still a little worried about how speeding things up will affect my future. I don't know anything about the rules and how the politics work in the future. I mean some of the movies I have watched about possible time travels are a little scary. For example, in one of the movies, you were only allowed to travel into the past or future to help yourself, but only a certain amount. If you went over what was allowed then there were big problems to face when you got back to your own time. So tell me a little about this kind of thing." I requested.

"Well, there isn't that much to tell. In

our time - mmm, your future, the only thing we are not allowed to do is mix or change who will be in office - politics, as you call It." he said.

"You mean you can come back and make yourself better off? I mean change your material value?" I asked, really needing to know if what I was thinking of doing wasn't going to get my future self in trouble.

"Now you have it." he answered quickly with a big smile.

"I really need to think about it a little more." I said, thinking of *'maybe asking the same question to Jack from the travel room on States Street.'*

"Ok, but don't wait too long. I want to be able to teach you everything you need to learn before I have to go back." he urged.

"Is there a way to get in touch with you when I make up my mind?" I asked.

"It will be easier for me to get back in touch with you." he said, "Shall I leave all the supplies with you here, while you figure it all out, or do you want me to take them back with me?" he asked.

"No, you can leave them here for right now. I am thinking of taking maybe a few lessons from you anyway. I'm just not sure as to how many right now." I answered as he got up and headed for the door.

We shook hands and he when down the hall in a hurry. I began to wonder if he was worried about running across the other traveler he thought he had seen earlier.

'I have a few hours free tomorrow, maybe I can go over and talk to Jack. Maybe he can shed some light on all this. I hope.' my thoughts trailed off as the phone rang.

"Hello," I said answering the phone.

"Hi Rita, So tell me what has happened since I talked to you last." said Nell.

"Oh, Hi Nell," I said with a laugh. "Well, you will never guess who just left my house."

I related all that had just happened and we had to laugh at all the crazy places this adventure had led us so far. And I have to say so far, because tomorrow? Well who knew? My whole life was turning around and around in my head and was so turned upside down that I often wondered what to do next, Like Now.

With my head still spinning I said "Good Bye." to Nell and sat down for the last of my morning coffee.

"Anna, it looks like I 'm going to have to go to the store soon." I told her.

She meowed with delight, because she loved going for walks with me.

I looked at my watch, "Oh my, it is already late afternoon. If we are going to the store, we should get going here pretty quickly. That way we can have something different for dinner, other than what I had planned." I said looking down at Anna.

She meowed as if to understand, made a few circles and headed for the door.

"Ok, let me change shoes and grab my wallet." I said heading for the bedroom.

When we got back from the store, and had eaten dinner, my mind started straying back to the "what ifs" while I washed the dinner dishes. *'I planned to go visit Jack tomorrow after work and ask him if he knew the answers to my questions and if not maybe he can find out without causing himself problems.'* "Oh my. What a dilemma. I need to know what is the safest for all of us." I caught myself saying aloud.

Anna came running to me and meowed as if to ask if there was anything she could help with.

"I was just thinking out loud again baby girl. There's nothing for you to worry about." I said stooping down to pet her. "You're such a good girl. Well, dishes are done and the kitchen is clean. Let's go watch a little TV.

'I need to find something to watch to get my mind off all the crazy things that have been

happening the last few weeks' I though as I sat down on the couch. As I flipped through the channels I could clearly see there wasn't anything worth watching so I started going through the movies that I had. But, I didn't see anything there that would work either. "Well baby girl looks like we are watching the news and then going to bed early."

Anna sat there on the couch with me and put her head on my lap and cuddled up during the news.

Just as the news ended, Anna ran into the bedroom, jumped on to the bed and curled up on her pillow.

I got ready for bed and after laying down my eyes wouldn't stay closed. *'Oh my gosh, if I don't sleep soon I will be so tired tomorrow, and I really need to go talk to Jack'.*

Before I knew it the sun came streaming through my bedroom window as if to say, "you have a lot to do. Get out of that bed."

Anna was already awake and

meowing for something to eat. I didn't get up quickly enough to suit her and she was soon in my face making sure I was awake.

"Okay baby girl, I'm awake and getting up. I looked at the clock and there was another ten minutes before the alarm was set to go off.

"I think we will have scrambled eggs this morning. Do you agree?" I asked looking down at Anna.

She gave a long meow and put her paws together on my knee. Then ran over and sat on the chair so she could see everything I did.

Since we were up early I could take my time in getting ready for work and had time to straighten the apartment before leaving.

Just as I finished I looked at the clock and saw it was time to gather up my things and Anna and head out to meet George.

"You be a good girl today and stay out of trouble." I said while giving Anna a hug and placing her on the banister and going to catch the bus.

"Hi George, are you running late today?" I asked.

"No, why?" he asked.

"I got up early today and was standing there for what seemed like a very long time." I said while laughing.

"Well there is your answer. Getting up early will do that to you." He said joining in the laughter. "You look a little worried about something. Can you tell me?" he asked.

"Not now, maybe later." I said as I started for the bench seat Nell was setting on.

"Hi Nell." I said as I sat down next to her.

'Okay spill the beans, what's up?" she asked.

Chapter 20

"Oh I need to go talk to Jack today and see if I can figure out the best way to handle all of this. I mean with the art teacher showing up four years early it seems it may cause trouble all the way around." I said trying to explain.

"Okay, now I'm lost. What do you think will happen if you were to start painting now instead of later?" she asked.

"Well if I was to start painting these kinds of pictures now then what would be the reason for me to come back later? And if I was to paint them now, they would have my name on them and not Anna's. And if she hadn't come back then I would have never thought about painting. So it is kind of like which came first the chicken or the egg. Would I have started painting if she hadn't shown up or would I have just kept going the way I have for the rest of my life and ended up in the same apartment in the same area till I died?" I explained.

"Oh! I see what you mean. What a mess." answered Nell even more puzzled.

"And besides, I just got to thinking. How did he know where I lived? I didn't tell him my address and Anna didn't meet him while she lived here." I said.

"So I plan to go see Jack after work today and see if he has anything that may help me figure out all of this. Or just maybe he can get a message to Anna and ask her what she thinks I should do." I said.

"That sounds like a good idea." Nell agreed.

"Here's my stop. I will call you later tonight." I said as I started for the door.

"Bye George." I yelled as I stepped off the bus.

Work started off slow but got faster and crowded as the day went on. Then about ten minutes before it was time for me to clock out, Jack walked in and sat down at the corner booth.

I went over thinking about asking him if we could talk when I got off work.

He just looked up at me and said. "I know, I was told to come and see if I could help. Meanwhile a cup of coffee would be nice."

"Good, thank you." I said as I turning to go get the coffee. There were a few others that needed refills at this point. I looked at the clock and I had two more minutes and maybe, just maybe I could get all of this settled in my mind.

I gave Jack his coffee and walked back behind the counter and took my time pulling off my apron and putting things away. Charlie came out of the back room just as I put my apron in the laundry.

"So you're off now? He asked.

"Yes but I will be here for a few more minutes. I need to talk to Jack." I explained.

I got myself a small soda and sat down at the table across from Jack. After explaining to him all that had happened since Anna had left he just sat there for a few minutes and starred into his coffee.

"Yep, it sounds like we have a problem." he finally said.

It seemed like forever before he said anything.

"So do you have any ideas? I mean I hadn't really given painting much thought before Anna came back because I always had to work just to pay the bills I have. Something like that just seemed so out of reach. So if she hadn't come back I may never have gotten into painting. That is problem number one and number two is that her art teacher has also came back in time to get me started painting four years early. And number three, if I were to start painting now it would have my name on the painting and that would make me in competition with myself later in life." I explained.

"Well, I am thinking, maybe only take about four lessons from her teacher while he is here and that is it till you meet him again four years from now. And you can sign them Anna May because they will just be the earlier works she /you painted before you came back. Besides, an alias is used by a lot of artist." he whispered so as not to be heard by anyone sitting close by.

I breathed a sigh of relief. "That sounds like a good plan. Gee I am glad you came by. All of this was driving me up the wall and I was getting more and more confused the more I thought about it. But I am wondering how he knew where I lived. I didn't tell him." I said.

"Well I need to get back to my station. I will see if I can get more information for you. I am the one in charge 24/7 that is why we have everything set up the way we do. I can only take a couple of hours off at a time. I enjoyed seeing the picture and talking with you. Maybe I can come by to eat one of these days." he said getting up to leave. "I will give you a call if I find out anything." he added.

"Okay, and yes please do come by when you can." I said taking our dishes back behind the counter.

"I thought you were off work." Charlie said with a big grin.

"I am and George will be here in a few minutes. I'm ready and waiting for him. I'm going home soon enough." I said laughing.

When Master Bastrono came back to given me my first lesson, he seemed very nervous. He showed me the basics and painted a picture himself while I watched. Before he left he had me look out my door to make sure no one else was around. I thought that alone was very strange. But he made arrangement to come back in a few days to show me a little more. This went on several times and then he stopped coming.

A few weeks later I went back to the art shop where Anna had bought her supplies and bought a few books to help me learn a little more.

I often found myself wondering what happen to Anna's teacher but as time pasted other things took my attention. Then one day…

"Hey Rita, a man named Jack stopped in to see you. He said he would come back later." Steffy said as I came through the door.

"Did he say anything other than he would be back?" I asked.

"No, but he is a good tipper." She said laughing.

"Okay thanks." I said hoping it would be while I was still at work. I wanted to let him know what I had been doing.

'Everything is going well and the crowds were still showing up to see the painting after all these many months. I don't mind. Life is better than ever. I got the raise and was working more hours per week. I figure by the end of the four years I will have saved enough to move to California. I don't know about living in San Francisco, I've heard it's real expensive.'

The clanking of dished brought me back to the present.

Charlie had decided to make a few more change to The Rooster now since business had gotten good. Now from about 4:30 P.M. we were to dress each table with a table cloth with a small vase of flowers and the silverware was to be wrapped in a cloth napkin.

I just finished dressing the last table when Steffy caught my attention. I looked up just in time to see Jack sit down at the table across from Anna's painting. I can't call it my painting because I haven't learned that much about painting yet.

I nodded to Jack and he nodded back. I walked a little closer to where Charlie was talking to Fred about the dinner menu.

He looked up from the menu. "Charlie I'm going to take a ten min break now while it is slowed down, if that's ok. I need to talk to Jack." I explained.

"You only have another twenty-five on the clock, but ok if you think you must." He said with a scowl and then with a big grin.

"Thanks." I said as I walked away.

I took off my apron and walked over and sat down at Jack's table.

Steffy was putting the silverware on the tables and when she got a little closer I reached out and grabbed her apron. Then looked at Jack, "Something to drink or eat?" I asked.

"A coffee, please." he said looking at Steffy who was now standing next to me.

"A small soda for me." I said giving her my Cheshire smile.

"Sure." came her answer with a giggle.

"We need to talk about the things that have been happening since Anna left." I said breaking the silence.

"Okay, you first. Did you take any lessons from her old teacher?" he asked.

"I took one real lesson then he never came back. But I have bought a few books and found a few more at the library. So I am trying to teach myself as much as I can till I see him in four years. Maybe he won't uh." I couldn't find the word I was looking for.

"Maybe he won't feel as scary or weird?" asked Jack.

"Yeah there was something about him that made my cat's hair stand on edge too." I said with a chuckle.

"Well I think that part is taken care of." Jack said with a little power behind it.

"What happened?" I asked leaning

forward to keep others from hearing too much.

"He was picked up on fraud charges. It seems he was working out a way to take credit for some of Anna's other paintings which will soon be found and thought to be earlier than the ones she just sold." he said laughing. "Confused yet?" he asked.

"Well they are earlier painting." I said "Timeline wise." I added joining him in laughter. "Anyway what is happening with Master Bastrono?" I asked.

"Oh, he had to give back all of the money he has made off anything that didn't belong to him and then he was fined twice the amount he had collected. AND he is permanently ban from any time journeys or jumps of any kind.

"Wow, then I won't have to worry about him showing up anywhere other than where he is to really be at the time he is to be there?" I asked to just make sure I hear all of this right.

"That's right. No more worries about him pushing himself into your life at the wrong time." he confirmed.

"Oh good" I said giving a sigh of relief. "To me that is good news. And that will give me time to study my older self's thinking for the process it took to paint like this." I said laying my hand out on the table toward Anna's painting. "I started a saving's account when I got my raise so I will have enough money to go to San Francisco in a little less than four years." I said feeling proud of myself.

"That sounds like a good idea." Jack said looking over my head at the clock. "I had better get back, but I wanted to let you know what had happened and keep you up on what I had found out."

We got up and I gathered his cup and my glass and we walked together to the front door where he paid for his coffee and left.

"Is Jack a new boyfriend or what?" Steffy probed.

"No just a good friend of the family." I informed her. "I can see that the dinner crowd hasn't started coming in yet so I have time to help in the kitchen a little before I meet George and go home." I added.

George walked in just as I finished washing the potatoes. "Here you go Fred. They are all clean and ready for you. George just walked in so I have to get ready to go home." I said walking back to the front of the café.

"Hi George, are you early or on time tonight?" I asked with a smile.

"I am just right. Not too early and not late, so just right." He said with a chuckle. "I have time for a coffee though." He added.

"I figured that." I said putting a cup

of coffee in front of him. I then started

gathering my things and getting ready to

get on the bus.

Enjoy other Books
by
Lauresa Tomlinson

Chapter Books

Crazy déjà vu -(pt. 2) Not Again

The Turning Stone

My Interview With a Fairy

Secretly Special - You too may be special too

There is an Alien in My Cereal

Elayta's Adventures in Space and Time
(pt 1) We Came to Visit
(pt 2) We Meet at Last
(pt 3) What Times May Be

Picture Books

Cats in Charge

Sleepy Time Baby Bear

Munchie and Goldie - Most Unlikely Friends

Others

Studies of Life -

Poetry, Love Sonnets and Thoughts

Expressive Tree People

Soon

Under the Pear Tree

The Turning Stone is about a young boy that is bullies. He finds a way out of that and shares the story of "The Ice Crossing" to his classmates.

Secretly Special is about four children that

are tease because of their physical appearance.
How they overcome the teasing and become
the school heroes.

**Elaytay's Adventures in Space and
Time** is about a young 16yr old female space
cadet and her adventures in Space and Time.

My Interview With a Fairy is about a
young girl that gets the chance to become a
near fairy and have all of her questions (over
60+) answers. Then chance to meet a Rubump.

There's an Alien in My Cereal is about a
young boy and Alien that finds out you can't
believe everything you hear about people you
don't know.

Sleepy Time Baby Bear is a baby bear
that finds it hard to fall asleep. Find out what
that special thing was that helped.

**Munchie and Goldie – Most Unlikely
Friends** is about a forest squirrel and a fantail
goldfish that find out you can be best friends
no matter your differences.

Expressive Tree People is a picture book
of strange but odd and funny characters
found in the Northern Forest of California

**Studies of Life – poetry, Love Sonnets
and Thoughts** is a collection of poems,
sonnets and thoughts that could have you
asking why or what?

There are more coming
Under the Pear Tree – is another
adventure with Amy and is part of My
Interview With a Fairy. It starts at her
Grandparents house.